I0536836

CHANCE
OF A LIFETIME
AN ANDERSON BROTHERS STORY

CHANCE OF A LIFETIME

AN ANDERSON BROTHERS STORY

MARISSA CLARKE

For Laine
Who gave me a real-life happily ever after.

Chapter One

Gen took a long pull on her beer, perversely enjoying her wallow in self-pity. It was a luxury she never allowed herself. Today, though, was different. All her buttressing against any show of weakness or self-doubt over the years seemed wasted, as did the protective cocoon she'd erected to appease her family. Today had brought home just how misdirected her entire life had been to date.

Sally, the receptionist for the recording studio, had been twenty-six—only one year older than her. *Boom. Done. Just like that.* Dead with no warning in a freak accident.

She downed the rest of her beer in harsh gulps and set the glass on the tiled bar. At least Sally had *lived* before she'd died. More than Gen could say for herself.

"Hot guy at two o'clock," Sherry, her best friend and coworker at Decibels Sound Studio, whispered from the barstool next to her. "Oooh. He's hella fine. Same guy as before. All tall and lean and badass broody."

"Why don't you go say hi?" Gen suggested, not ready to give up her self-indulgent pity party.

"Another beer?" Andy asked from behind the bar as he swept her glass away with a staccato scrape across the rough surface.

She liked the bartender. His voice had a musical quality and he smelled of Old Spice deodorant—she knew because it was what her brother used—and whiskey. Today, the whiskey scent wasn't as pronounced, but it was early yet. By the end of his shift, he would sport at least an ounce of various liquors. The smell of alcohol reminded her of someone else—someone she didn't allow herself to think about anymore.

She ran her fingers across the small, jagged tiles of the bar and pulled a pretzel from the paper-lined plastic basket situated between her and Sherry. "Sure. Another beer would be great."

The crunching of the pretzel drowned out the click and fizzle of Andy pulling the tap on her beer, but not the appreciative yummy noises Sherry made with regard to the guy she'd mentioned earlier.

"Don't look now, but he's watching you."

Gen snorted at her friend's joke. Sherry was the only one who felt comfortable enough to kid with her about a topic everyone else considered taboo. "Don't worry, I'm not looking."

"Here you go." Andy set her glass down in front of her, gently pushing it against her hand.

"Who's the guy at the corner table?" Sherry asked.

"Oh, that's the doctor. He's been hanging out here on Tuesday nights for a while." Glasses clinked as he moved them behind the bar.

Sherry shifted on her stool with a rustle of fabric. "Tuesdays. That's *our* night here. A *doctor*. Did you hear that, Gen?"

He laughed. "No. That's our nickname for him because he always orders a Dr Pepper. No booze. Ever."

Rubbing her finger around the rim of the glass, Gen sighed. No alcohol would probably have been a good choice for her tonight, considering her mood.

Andy leaned close enough for the air to move across her face and arms. "You okay?"

Funny. That was probably the number one question people asked her. And she always answered the same way. Hundreds—no, thousands—of times, she'd answered yes. But she was lying. She wasn't okay. She'd never been okay. She never *would* be…not unless something changed. Unless she *made* it change before it was too late and she ended up like that poor girl at the receptionist desk who choked on a mint.

Nothing reckless. Nothing dangerous or daring. Simply a mint. Just like that.

"No, I'm not okay," she answered. "I'm horrible, in fact. Never been worse."

"We lost a coworker," Sherry explained. "It was unexpected."

Andy cleared his throat. "I'm sorry."

"Me, too. She was supersweet."

She regretted not hanging out with her more. Sally had asked her to go out after work several times, but she'd always declined. She'd been too busy keeping to her routine. Following her brother's wishes. Playing it safe. Never stepping outside her circle of safety.

Safety. For what? Sally was a fun-loving, outgoing girl who had recently become engaged. And she died because she choked on a mint, not because she did something dangerous like ski down some uncharted vertical slope or jump out of an airplane—or in the case of Gen, simply cross the freaking street.

Which just went to show, no matter how careful she was, no matter how protective her brother was of her, something unexpected could come along and end it all in the blink of an eye.

No more. From now on, no more playing it safe. She reached to get her purse off the next stool and accidentally bumped her cane, which fell to the ground with a metallic *clang.* When Sherry made to retrieve it, she stilled her with a hand on her shoulder. "I've got this." After righting the cane, she rooted in her purse until she found what she was looking for. She flattened the scrap of paper on the bar and slid back onto her stool.

"What is that?" her friend asked.

Gen closed her eyes and remembered how excited she'd been in high school when she created this. Life had so many possibilities at fifteen. Funny how ten years could turn that around. "It's my bucket list."

The paper crinkled as Sherry picked it up. "What's on it?"

She didn't even need to read it to know what it said. "Things I intend to do as soon as possible. Starting with number one right now."

The list had sat dormant for ten years. But not anymore. No more waiting for a mint to off her.

Sherry squealed through her nose like she did at the studio when she was really excited. "You know I can't read braille. What's first on the list?"

A smile stretched across her face. "Number one: Kiss a total stranger."

Chapter Two

Once Sherry stopped squealing and clapping, and the list was tucked carefully back inside her purse, Gen took a deep breath and a fortifying swallow of beer.

Yep. She was really going to do this, and no big brother or an overabundance of caution or fear was going to get in her way. "Where's the doc?"

"He's in the corner still." Sherry rotated her forty-five degrees plus a little more.

"Obstacles?"

"Nothing right now. Do you want your cane?"

"No. If I'm clear, I'm going hands-free."

And for a moment, her heart seemed to stop beating. This was way out of character for her. As if sensing her doubt, Sherry leaned closer. "Good idea. As smokin' hot as this guy is, you're definitely going to want your hands free."

The encouragement did the trick and her heart kicked in again. "How far away?"

"Twenty feet, max," Andy said.

"Standing or sitting?"

Sherry giggled. "Sitting on a stool. His face is perfect height for a lip-lock."

For a moment, a lump rose in her throat. *Nuh-uh.* She'd suppressed all signs of life for years now. *No chickening out. Not ever again.* After another deep breath, she raked her bangs out of her face. "Get me within six feet of him and point me in the right direction," she instructed her friend, who immediately offered her elbow.

Consciously loosening her death grip on Sherry's arm, Gen took a step forward, and then another until she counted ten steps, which should put her within five or so feet of him.

"Straight ahead," Sherry mumbled under her breath then pulled her hand away.

Gen tilted her head and listened, but picked up nothing other than her friend's retreating steps and the regular sounds of the bar early on a Tuesday night. "What's up, Doc?" she asked, finally.

No answer. Not even breathing. Odd. Usually, people answered her—sometimes almost yelling because of a bizarre prevalent assumption that blind people must not be able to hear either.

With one arm bent in front of her face at eye level and the other making slow sweeps straight out in front, she shuffled closer to where she was told he was sitting on a stool.

A slight rise in temperature registered through her fingertips, indicating she was close, and then contact. Soft cotton jersey over hard muscle.

Damn.

Skimming lightly, her second hand joined the first in a sweep over the surprisingly solid planes of his chest. And still, he said nothing.

Laying her palms flat on his pecs, she could feel his rapid, strong heartbeat, which accelerated by the second. He might not be speaking, but he was certainly surprised. The quiet type. She liked that.

She trailed her fingers higher, over his clavicle, up the sides of his neck, where soft hair brushed the tops of her hands. Long hair. She liked that, too. And his smell was fabulous. Minty and clean with an overlay of Gain laundry detergent—the same one she used.

Slight stubble like what would happen over the course of a day covered his angular jaw, and her thumbs roamed over full, soft, parted lips.

Shit! What was she doing? She was standing in a bar fondling the face of a perfect stranger, that's what. Completely perfect, she concluded, as his rapid breaths blew across her fingers. Her hands trembled and a spike of longing pierced her control.

For a fleeting moment, she almost stepped away, but then remembered how carefree she'd been a decade ago when she'd created her bucket list. She could live that way again, waking up every morning excited for what the world would bring, rather than simply plodding through the days, ticking off tasks on her schedule, counting steps, and making her family happy.

It was time for a change, and this was the first step to taking her life back. This kiss. Right now.

At some point during her internal deliberations, he had stood, making her reach up in order to keep her fingers on his lips. She slid her hands down his neck to the top of his shoulders and pushed hard until he sat on the stool again, then caught his jaw in her hands.

For a moment she paused, and her customary caution crept in.

No. No more playing it safe. This was it. Her first step to a new life, and hell or high water, she wouldn't wimp out now. She covered his mouth with hers, surprised by the softness of his lips compared to the hard muscles of his chest. As if frozen, he didn't react to her mouth moving across his. But when she ran her tongue along the seam of his lips, he made the first sound since this whole business started—a cross between a whimper and a groan—and placed a hand in the center of her back, splaying his fingers wide between her shoulder blades. Then he tilted his head and finally kissed her back.

And, man, oh, man, could he kiss. Like nothing she'd experienced before—not that she'd kissed a ton of guys, but she'd kissed a few. Enough to know this wasn't a garden-variety encounter.

She ran her fingers through his soft hair and scraped her nails across his scalp. This time when he made a noise, it was more of a growl, filling her from head to toe with a heady buzzing electric sensation, culminating in a warm flush in her belly. He pulled back breathing heavily, like her.

No more caution or careful planning. From this point forward, she wanted to feel like this. Alive and sensual and needed—not needy. Though honestly, she *was* needy, but in a physical way—not an emotional, dependent way.

"Don't stop," she said, tightening her grip in his hair. He responded by wrapping his arms around her, pulling her between his thighs until their bodies touched and his hard bulge pressed against the front of her jeans.

His tongue stroked hers in a rhythm her body recognized instinctually, and that hot flush in her belly happened again.

Yes. This was living. This was who she was, not some timid, fractured creature reliant on others to assure her safety and happiness.

On and on, the kiss continued, their tongues tangling as their bodies heated until she was sure she'd combust right there in the bar in front of everyone…

Oh, damn.

Yeah, they were in front of people, making out like horny teenagers. *Double damn.*

And as the world came back into focus, punctuated by clinks of glasses and nineties music, the buzzing in her body receded, and she took a reluctant step back. The cool air swirled where his hot body had just been, making her shudder. What should she do now? Was she supposed to say thank you? Or maybe, "Holy shit, buddy, you can kiss!"

Was there a protocol for addressing a stranger she'd walked up to and kissed? Probably not, so she simply cut her losses and walked away, heading straight back in the direction from which she'd come.

"Genny."

She stopped dead in her tracks, pulse hammering in her ears. No one called her that. At least not in the last ten years. She swallowed hard. *No. It couldn't possibly be…* His face was too angular and he was too tall and muscular to be… *Chance Anderson.* Just saying the name in her head made gooseflesh rise on her arms.

He'd been only seventeen back then, still just a boy. This was a man.

And he smelled nothing like Chance, who had been cloaked in cigarette smoke and suntan lotion, and reeked of adventure and freedom.

This guy, with all his sharp angles and hard planes, smelled of toothpaste and clean clothes. His scent was refined, but his kisses certainly weren't. She raised her fingers to her lips. God. Had she just kissed her big brother's best friend? Surely not…

"Genny," he said again in his rich, nuanced saxophone voice, and as he moved within reach, recognition funneled through her in a sickening trickle all the way down to her toes. The voice was almost the same. She'd know it anywhere.

How could this have happened? Of the thousands of people she could have randomly kissed in this city, it had to be Chance.

And as instinctively as her body had responded to his kiss, her mind and heart reacted to his voice. She reached out and laid her palm on his cheek, and then, with no prelude, she drew back and slapped him as hard as she could.

The asshole.

Chapter Three

It had taken all of Chance's self-control to not block her strike, and then even more restraint to remain perfectly still as Genny, brow furrowed, flapped her hand. As bad as it had stung his face, it was no surprise it had hurt her—which brought him no joy whatsoever.

Her mahogany-brown hair was pulled back in a ponytail that reached her shoulder blades, with a fringe of bangs framing her face. He could see the outline of her lace bra through the pale pink V-neck T-shirt under a blazer the same rich chocolate color as her eyes. That, in combination with her tight jeans with designer holes at the knees, made her all kinds of casual sexy.

Without a word, she walked toward her friend with the short skirt and spiked black hair, who helped her gather her things and led her out the door while he stood there dumbfounded.

He had no idea what had set her off. Honestly, right up until the moment she slapped the shit out of him, he thought she'd known who he was. If he'd had a shred of common sense or decency, he'd have slipped out of reach before she kissed him in the first place. Clearly, he had neither of those attributes.

And what the fuck was that about anyway? Who did she think she was kissing if not him?

He touched a finger to his lips. She'd tasted of beer, and salt, and…

Holy shit, shit, shit. He'd kissed *Genny*—the most taboo woman in the world. Genevieve Elizabeth Richards—his best friend's little sister. His stomach plummeted to his feet. Walter would kill him for this if he found out.

It was imperative his friend never found out. Which meant he had to talk to Genny before she got to her brother.

"Hey, buddy. Hold on a minute," the bartender called as he strode toward the door. "I need to talk to you."

Not nearly as badly as Chance needed to talk to Genny. Not even slowing, he continued toward the exit hoping he could catch her before she got too far away. "If you don't stop, I'm calling the cops and telling them you're a creeper stalking a blind girl."

Son of a bitch. Just short of the door, he turned and faced the guy. The cops wouldn't believe that for a second, but the last thing he needed was a scene. He'd broken his promise to Walter and he'd fucked up—again. He needed to keep things low-key and make this right. He held his hands up in a gesture of surrender. "We're cool. No need for that."

The guy grabbed a towel and wiped the area Genny and her friend had just vacated and gestured for him to sit.

Chance slid onto the stool, fighting the urge to glance over his left shoulder at the door. She was getting farther away by the second. His only shot at talking to her was to catch her on the street.

"So, what's your story?" the bartender asked.

"I don't have one."

His eyes narrowed. "I'm not good with letting you follow her."

The guy's tenacious overprotectiveness was a pain in the ass, but Chance had to admire his loyalty to Genny. He acted as if he had an interest in her more than that of customer, which shouldn't be a surprise. She was a smart, beautiful woman. Of course she'd have guys after her. He tamped down the unexpected jealousy accompanied by hot prickles up his neck.

"You clearly know her. At least you know her name," the bartender continued, pitching the rag aside and crossing his arms over his chest. When Chance didn't respond, the guy pushed harder. "Who is Gen to you?"

"Who is she to *you*?" His voice came out louder and harsher than intended. It was like his limbic system had totally overridden reason and control. Like the old days…

The guy met his eyes directly. "She's a friend."

"Same here…well, we used to be friends."

The bartender arched an eyebrow. After a moment, he grabbed a glass, filled it with ice, then popped the top on a can of Dr Pepper and poured it. "There's a long story here, isn't there? One that will explain why you've been hanging out here on Tuesday nights for a couple of months."

"Yeah, a very long story. Too long."

He slid the glass in front of Chance and placed his hands wide on the bar. Not threatening, per se, but definitely making it clear he was ready to make threats if need be. "You're not going to follow her. I have all night. Settle in and tell me a story, Doc. I'm a great listener."

But Genny's big brother, Walter, wasn't a great listener. He never had been. And if she got to him before Chance cleared the air with her, it would be bad. Really bad. Just like a decade ago. "I met Genny around twenty years back, when I was in second-grade Little League with her brother."

The guy relaxed and placed a fresh basket of pretzels in front of him.

"The boys on the team were teasing Walter about his little sister." Chance closed his eyes and could see it as if it were yesterday. Her mom had been watching practice from the bleachers, but got up to go do something. The boys were calling Genny "weirdo" and worse. Walter, a good head shorter than the other boys, did nothing to stand up for his little sister, who was sitting alone on the bench with a ratty doll rocking back and forth singing to it. Chance's heart broke when she stopped singing and turned her head to listen to the boys' taunts. She continued to rock, but he knew she'd heard because a tear slid down her face and landed on the doll. She brushed it away from the doll's face and told it to not listen to the mean boys. That she was a beautiful, smart doll and should never cry.

At five, she'd had more wisdom and strength than the little shits who had mocked her. Sometimes, even now, he'd see that moment in his sleep and wake up in a cold sweat, wanting to kick the world's ass for being so heartless.

Taking a deep breath, he loosened his grip on his glass and set it gently on the bar.

A waitress dropped off a ticket and the bartender drew a draft beer and handed it to her, then turned his attention back to him. "And so you defended him, put the bullies in their places, and the two of you bonded and became fast friends."

"No. I defended *her* and got the shit beaten out of me." He took a sip of his soda. "We bonded in the ER waiting room when his mom took me to get the stitches over my right eye."

The guy winced and extended his hand. "I'm Andy, by the way."

"Chance Anderson." After a quick shake, he glanced at

the door. He'd never catch her now. Walter was going to be royally pissed off—and for good reason.

"Why do you need to talk to her so bad?"

"To warn her off telling her brother about the...what just happened. I promised him that I wouldn't interfere with her life." He ran a hand through his hair. "I was simply making sure she was okay. She never even knew I was here." Neither had Walter, and he hoped to keep it that way.

Andy barked a laugh. "Well, she knows now! It's pretty random you were the one she selected to kiss."

"Random. Yeah." He shook his head and drank the rest of his soda. "Incredibly random."

"So big brother asked you to keep an eye on her?"

"Something like that." Chance and Walter weren't as close as they had been in high school, but they still met up a couple of times a month to run in the park. They never talked about Genny. Ever. But two months ago that changed. As they jogged past East Green, Walter said his sister had moved out of their parents' house and into her own apartment while he was out of town on business. Chance had never seen his friend so worried.

Wanting to be sure she was okay, Chance waited outside her building in Midtown the next day until she left work, and then followed her to this bar. He took the corner seat, telling himself he was only making sure she was safe, but he knew at that moment, he wouldn't be able to stay away. Walter would blow a gasket if he discovered that Chance hung out in a bar every Tuesday to catch a glimpse of his little sister.

"You seem like a good guy, Chance. So what if I tell you I know where she is right now?"

He tried not to let his excitement at that news show. He'd been coming to the bar every week, but had never allowed himself to seek her out beyond that. "I'd be very grateful if you'd give me that information."

"There's a price."

"There always is."

"I'll tell you where they went if you put in a good word for me with her friend, Sherry."

He had to be kidding. Genny had just slapped him and stormed out mad. No word from him would be good. "Sure. No problem."

Chapter Four

On step thirty-seven, Gen knew she was within half a block of the corner. Even this late at night, the traffic on Broadway was heavy and loud. "Chance Anderson is a total jackwagon, I tell you."

Sherry barked a laugh and fell into step beside her. "He's a hot AF total jackwagon."

"Don't let his looks fool you. I don't," Gen said.

Sherry snorted.

Enjoying her mini rant, she continued. "He's a royal asshat. All bow down to King Asshat," she shouted, knowing full well that nobody in Times Square gave a shit.

They reached the corner, and Sherry busted out laughing. "I volunteer! I'd totally genuflect before that guy. Holy shit, Gen, he's gorgeous. And those eyes! The bluest I've ever seen. I can't believe you actually know him. And damn, girl, you guys were really into it. I'm going to have to go home and find some batteries after watching that."

Why did the guy she kissed have to be Chance? She couldn't even get reckless down right. She heard the traffic shift, and she tapped the curb with her cane.

"All clear," Sherry said, lightly touching her elbow as they crossed the street.

When they'd first started hanging out together, Sherry had hovered too much and had pulled her around like she couldn't find her way on her own. Sighted people tended to think being blind was like a sighted person wearing a blindfold. So not true. Her other senses were fine-tuned and came close to making up for the lack of sight. She could tell where alcoves, alleys, and doors were from the sound of her cane taps rebounding off the buildings as she walked. She could even tell what material the walls were made of from the taps. Wood sounded different from glass, and metal sounded nothing like brick. She was good at predicting age and gender from footfalls in passing, and with her adaptive technology on her phone, she could use apps for location and even to identify objects.

Before long, her new friend realized how well she functioned and backed off, treating her like a person, not a disability, which is exactly what she needed—especially in light of her parents and brother still treating her like she was helpless and hopeless. Something Chance had never done, which was why his betrayal had hurt so much.

Fuck that. Fuck *him*. She inhaled a deep breath, taking in the familiar city smells. Car fumes, assorted food odors, and a tinge of garbage from the late-night pickup.

Yeah, "fuck him" was right. That was the problem. That's exactly what she wanted to do—what she'd wanted to do from the moment she knew what that word meant.

By high school, she was hopelessly in love with her brother's best friend. He was the only one who had ever treated her like she wasn't blind. He let her go everywhere with him—to concerts, to movies, even on his family's yacht. He'd never kissed her or acted romantic, but in her adolescent, romantic mind, that was because he was noble and polite. It wasn't until later, after he'd disappeared without a word, that she realized the affection had been one-sided. If he'd considered her a friend at all, he would have answered her calls or at least said good-bye.

Her cane skittered across a fracture in the pavement and she slowed. She'd been an idiot back then to think Chance cared. He was almost three years older and never saw her as anything other than a little girl.

The pavement leveled out and she picked up her pace, sweeping her cane directly in front of her because of the number of people still out and about. It was one of the things she loved about living in New York City. She was never truly alone—which is how she'd felt for years after Chance disappeared without a word. And now, ten years later, here he was, probably still seeing her as that same little girl.

A hot wave passed through her at the memory of his body against hers as they kissed. He certainly hadn't kissed her like he thought she was a little girl.

Fuck him, she growled in her head.

Yeah…exactly.

"We're here."

Cool air scented with baked waffle cone and fresh cream washed over Gen's face as Sherry opened the door to the ice cream shop. Two beers and now ice cream meant an extra hot yoga class. Totally worth it, though.

Before they reached the counter, her phone rang. No doubt about who it was. Even if it weren't for the customized ring, she'd know it was her brother's routine evening call. "Hi, Walter. I'm fine."

"Are you home?" It was silent in the background, which meant he was still at the office or at his apartment.

"Almost."

"Why are you still out?"

Angry prickles crawled up her neck. When would he realize she wasn't a child? "I worked late." No way was she telling him the truth. He'd probably threaten to withhold trust money.

"Call me when you get to your apartment so I know you made it safely."

It was easier to agree than argue. Besides, she didn't want another conversation with her friend about how she needed to deal with her big brother. "Fine."

She slipped her phone into her bag as Sherry ordered a double-scoop mint chocolate chip ice cream cone. Gen got her usual single scoop cup of double fudge delight.

"So, what's next on your list after kissing a total stranger—or is that a do-over since he wasn't really a stranger?" her friend asked as they tucked into chairs in the corner.

"No do-overs." That kiss could never be topped. Her body thrummed with energy as her mind replayed the feel of his hands and mouth on her. "Next is a roller coaster." Which didn't seem nearly as daring or exciting as kissing Chance. But when she'd made the list at fifteen, it had held appeal.

Maybe because she'd envisioned herself doing it with her big brother's best friend, who would have certainly wrapped a protective arm around her in her vivid teen imagination.

She dug her spoon into her ice cream and pushed the image from her mind.

"Soooooooo, you gonna tell me about it?"

"Do I have a choice?"

"Not if you value your shins, because I'm going to move all your furniture around so you whack into stuff if you don't give me the scoop on the doc and why you dislike him so much."

She didn't dislike him. That was the problem. Even after all this time, part of her still longed for him, while another part wanted to let him know how much he'd hurt her. She swallowed hard and took a breath. He probably hadn't even thought of her after that horrible night. "I told you. Because he's a jerk."

"You can't get off that easily. Not this time. There's more to this. Spill."

She took a bite of her ice cream and thought about how to sum it up concisely. A protracted discussion of her teen crush would only make matters worse. "We used to hang out a lot, Walter, Chance, and me. Our parents were friends—still are."

She hadn't realized she'd drifted off into her memories until her friend cleared her throat theatrically.

"Walter had a lot of after-school commitments starting in middle school because of lacrosse practice, so often, it was just Chance and me hanging out. We were very close...or at least I thought we were." She took another bite, not even appreciating the smooth chocolate taste. "Walter treated me like a helpless blind sister. Chance...didn't. Ever. He treated me like..."

"A girlfriend?"

She sighed. "No. Like a regular person."

"Ah," her friend said, paper napkin rustling as she likely wiped her lips. "So why the slap instead of relocating that hot make-out session to your apartment where it belongs?"

Excitement and horror in equal parts flashed down her spine in prickly heat at the thought of Chance being in her apartment. "Because he..." How could she finish that sentence without sounding melodramatic? *Betrayed me* seemed too much, but was the truth. "Let me down."

"Still listening."

Shit. "We went to the harbor for New Year's Eve—Walter, Chance, me, and a neighbor of ours named Phoebe who Walter was hot for." She took another bite of ice cream. "I never really liked Phoebe. She was always talking the boys into doing stupid stuff."

"Like what?"

"Like breaking into my parents' liquor cabinet. Anyway, the four of us went to the harbor. It wasn't a date between Chance and me, but being only fifteen, it was as close as I'd come, and, well…I had a good imagination."

"So, you came on to him. That's understandable."

"No. I would never have done that. I…he…" She smoothed the top of her ice cream with the back of her spoon. "Well, I was intimidated and clueless. At that time, the three years he had on me seemed like decades. I had some romantic notion that if I had him alone at midnight without Walter and Phoebe, he'd kiss me to ring in the new year. I thought that was a rule—you had to kiss whomever you were with when the new year came in."

"Well, I'm glad that's not a rule, because you've spent the last three New Years' with me. I like you, hon, but not that way."

She laughed.

"Sorry," Sherry said. "I didn't mean to interrupt. Then what happened?"

She'd never forget that night. Everything changed because of it. *She* changed. She pushed her ice cream away and sighed. "We were playing Skee-Ball and I was desperate to get Chance alone. I convinced him to take me to the edge of a pier at the far end of the marina."

"Well, that was clever."

"I thought so at the time. It turned out to be a stupid mistake. When we got to the end, his phone rang and he told me I needed to go hang out with Walter for a few minutes because he had to do something—an errand. He said it would take less than five minutes."

"What was the errand?"

"I don't know. It didn't matter. In my fifteen-year-old

mind, the only thing that mattered was me."

"Hah! I'm still that way."

"No, you're not." Sherry was the kindest, most giving person she knew. "Anyway, I refused to go hang out with my brother. It had been hard to get Chance alone on the pier, and I was sure it wouldn't work again. I convinced him to just leave me there while he ran his quick errand. I scolded him for treating me like a little kid who needed a babysitter. I could tell he didn't want to leave me alone, but I was the whine master and he relented once I promised to sit down and not budge from the spot. I really wanted that kiss, and at the time, I thought I was as able as a sighted person."

"You are."

"Most of the time, yes, but I was in an unfamiliar place." She could almost smell the salty air and hear the laughter of people on the boardwalk and music from a live band.

"Still listening. Nothing slap-worthy yet."

Aware her friend was studying her, she consciously relaxed her face and arms. "Well, he'd promised it would take less than five minutes, but after half an hour, I got mad, imagining all kinds of crazy reasons he'd left me there." She still imagined all kinds of reasons. Over the years, she'd pondered every scenario from him leaving to avoid her, to his meeting up with a girl and forgetting about her until the next morning. "I also worried he wouldn't be back before midnight and I'd miss that kiss, so I decided to set out to find him. Show him I was like any other girl and not handicapped. The fireworks went off the moment I stood. I didn't have a cane because I wanted to look normal and cool and maybe make people think Chance was my date—maybe make him think it." She'd lived it over and over so many times in her head, it was like it had happened yesterday. Her breath caught as it played out in her mind. "The fireworks were loud and I became disoriented and headed the wrong direction, right off the side of the pier."

"In January."

"Technically, still December for a few minutes, but yeah. It was freezing. I tried to get out of the water, but couldn't. My down coat, boots, and heavy sweater were deadweight, so swimming was hard. If there was a ladder, I couldn't find it, and all the pilings were covered in barnacles, so I got cut up as I hung on."

"You must have been terrified."

"I was pretty freaked out. Hitting the water was a shock. Not finding a way out and being sliced up was worse. Eventually, some cops came and fished me out. I'd been in the water about fifteen minutes and everyone was worried about hypothermia. I also had a lot of gashes from the barnacles, so I was taken by ambulance to the hospital."

"Did Chance come in the ambulance with you?"

"No. That's the worst part. He didn't show up until the next day." Whatever reason he'd left her for had obviously been more important. Tears stung her eyes and she turned her head toward the door pretending to be interested in a family that entered the ice cream shop, making way more racket than seemed necessary for three people—maybe four if there was a kid being carried. With her heightened sense of hearing, she could identify number with excellent accuracy.

Sherry's foot tapped against the base of the table. "And?"

"And he didn't give any excuses or explanations as to why he didn't come directly to the hospital. I assumed he'd left to do something somewhere else or he was mad at me for not staying where I said I would. When he finally appeared, my parents ordered him to leave, but he didn't. Walter and Chance argued, and then he left. Tonight was the first time I've seen him since."

"And it was quite a reunion."

No kidding.

"There has to be more to that story." Sherry's chair scraped on the floor as she stood. The air stirred as she gathered her garbage from the table. "It makes no sense that he didn't come straight to the hospital, and I don't understand why he stopped talking to you. You're leaving something out."

It was too hard to explain. At the hospital, he and her big brother had talked about her like she wasn't even in the room—or worse, like she wasn't competent enough to be included in the conversation.

"She could have died!" Walter had yelled. "She's disabled. Blind. Helpless." He'd used every word she'd been denying for years, over and over until she'd wanted to scream. But she didn't. She'd lain in the hospital bed completely silent. Helpless, like she'd been labeled.

At fifteen years old, surrounded by her disapproving family, covered in stitches, and embarrassed at her reliance on sighted people, all she wanted was to be normal and independent. She'd thought Chance saw her that way, but he just took her brother's reprimand in silence, never once defending himself or her. He might as well have called her those things himself.

After that, Walter launched into a tirade about how careless Chance was and how he was always doing crazy shit. That he was a terrible influence. Her parents told the boys to take the discussion out of the room, probably because she was shaking at that point.

And then Chance left with Walter, muttering the only words he'd said directly to her since he arrived at the hospital, and the last words she'd heard from him in a decade. "I'm sorry, Genny."

Until tonight. That one word—"Genny"—was all it had taken to rip her heart wide open again. She bet he hadn't even looked back since he'd left her at the hospital. Never once felt the pain of her absence.

As if of its own accord, her palm pressed to her sternum where the old, familiar ache pounded.

"So, are Chance and your brother still friends?"

"They drifted apart for a while after that, but reconnected in law school. I'm not sure how close they are. Chance is a taboo topic with my brother—with my whole family, really. I kept track of him through news articles about his family or high school friends, though. He was always doing cool stuff. Climbing mountains, white-water rafting, skydiving. Even as early as sixth grade, he loved danger—which drove my family crazy." It drove her crazy, too, only in a different way.

For weeks after the hospital, she'd called and texted his number multiple times a day with no answer. Then, her attempts got further apart until she stopped calling altogether when she finally got his silent message loud and clear. *Leave me alone.*

Sherry touched her shoulder. "Sorry, Gen."

Not nearly as sorry as she was. Her entire life had been ripped out from under her that night. From that point forward, her family had helicopter hovered, never letting her go anywhere unchaperoned until two months ago, once she'd scraped enough money together from her job to rent her own apartment. Even then, she had to be sneaky and move out when Walter was out of town. But that wasn't going to be the end of her quest for independence.

"I'm taking the rest of the week off from work. I already turned in my vacation leave notice," she said, reaching for her cane propped against the table.

"Whoa. Vacation? That doesn't sound like you."

It didn't, but Sally's death was a game changer. "I'm on a mission. I'm going to knock out the bucket list."

The door opened, and she turned her head to listen but the outrageously loud family leaving drowned out whoever had entered.

"What else is on your bucket list?"

"Stuff I should have done a long time ago, but played it safe instead. Not anymore. Over the next week, I'm going to do all those things I've been wanting to do since high school."

"Like what? Oh my God! Tell me getting laid is on that list!"

She laughed. "The list is secret, but you'd approve. Daring and dangerous—at least it seemed to be when I was fifteen. Can you take some time off work to help me work through it?"

"I wish. I used up all my vacay days for that trip to Costa Rica, and I'm helping my sister move this weekend."

Her bubble of determination and enthusiasm deflated like a punctured balloon. She had figured Sherry would be her sidekick for this adventure. Clearly, she hadn't thought this out well enough. She'd acted impulsively, which always got her in trouble. Still, she was going to make this happen. "Well, I'll just have to do it alone." Which was next to impossible. She was savvy and totally able to navigate the city, but some of the things required a sighted person. Maybe she could hire someone... No. Sadly, she didn't make that kind of money working at Decibels, and since Walter watched her modest trust account like a hawk, he'd know she was up to something if she made a withdrawal. He'd swoop in to tell her that what she was doing was dangerous and put a stop to it.

Her friend sat back down. "I don't think I like the sound of this."

She inhaled to respond and froze when the scent of Gain and mint met her nose.

She sniffed twice, loudly for show. "Hey, Sher. Do you smell something?" She turned her face toward the door and wrinkled her nose dramatically. "I smell bullshit."

Her friend cleared her throat.

Rude wasn't her norm, but dammit, she was pissed. First the bar, now here. "It's hard to be full of something and not smell like it. Am I right?"

Chance laughed, which threw her a little because her entire body tightened and buzzed at the sound. It was like being a smitten fifteen-year-old all over again.

As he pulled back the chair next to her, across from Sherry, she put her hands in her lap so she wouldn't fidget—or worse, touch him. At this point, she wasn't sure whether she'd slap him or kiss him again. *I am so screwed.*

"What do you want, Chance?"

"To talk."

Sherry's chair scraped the floor as she stood. "Well, that's my cue to go, kids."

Gen grabbed her friend by the arm and yanked hard, forcing her back into her seat. "Please stay. This won't take long. Chance has a habit of taking off all of a sudden without a word."

"Genny, I—"

"Don't call me that. I go by Gen. Genny was someone else. Someone stupid."

There was a long, awkward silence before he spoke. "Gen. It's good to see you."

"Afraid I can't say the same. Can't see at all...but wait. You know that. You and Walter discussed that at length at the hospital. I'm disabled and helpless."

"I never said that."

"You never refuted it, either." *Jerk.* She took a shaky breath through her nose. *Delicious-smelling jerk.*

There was an excruciatingly long pause until Sherry cleared her throat again, then more silence followed. Gen pretended to be interested in finishing her ice cream, which was a melty mess—just like her insides. She had to get away from him before she couldn't. All those old feelings came back so hard and fast. It was as if her body didn't know he had betrayed her.

"Walter tells me you work at a sound studio. That's cool. It's the perfect job for you," he said, voice conversational and in complete opposition to how she was feeling at the moment.

"Yeah. Blind people hear well," she snapped. "When we're not busy being helpless, we hear stuff."

Sherry shifted in her chair, and for a moment she felt like the bitch she was playing out.

"I'm working for my family's business as the company lawyer."

"I know that. I overheard Walter telling my mom and dad a few years ago." She dropped the spoon in her cup and wiped her fingers with a napkin, then retrieved her cane and stood. "You're old news, Chance Anderson." Everything in her wanted to spend more time with him, but she'd imagined this meeting for a decade and it always ended the same way in her mind. She took a deep breath and uttered the words she'd imagined saying over and over. "See ya...or not."

As she gathered her trash from the table, cane propped against her side, a flush of disappointment washed through her. In her imagination, that line was always a triumphant blow delivered to her enemy. Instead, it just felt...lame—like her life in general. After pitching her cup, spoon, and napkin in the trash, she tapped her cane around the edge of the can, across the slick vinyl floor, and contacted the metal door threshold, but was stopped short by his next words.

"I need your help, Gen."

Now that wasn't in any of her imagined scenarios. Chance asking for assistance was nowhere on her radar.

She faced him, but said nothing.

"I understand you're mad at me for what happened on New Year's all those years ago. It still makes me sick to think of you in that water..."

Holy crap. He thought she was mad about the fall. It was all she could do to not laugh. The discomfort of the cold and stitches was nothing compared to his ripping her heart out. Clutching her cane in a death grip, she kept her voice low and controlled. "What do you want, Chance?"

"For you to not tell Walter we...that... Please don't tell him about the bar."

As if. Walter would never let her out of his sight if he knew she'd kissed a guy in a bar. "Do you really think I'd be stupid enough to tell your best friend from high school, who just happens to be my big brother, that you stuck your tongue in my mouth and groped my ass?"

His breath audibly hitched. "You mean the part where you walked up and practically jumped me—or rather jumped whomever you thought I was."

"Well, I sure as hell didn't think it was you."

"Clearly not."

"Now, kids. Let's play nice," Sherry said.

"He started it," Gen snapped, sounding just like the little girl he most certainly believed her to be.

"And I want to end it," he replied. "I was pretty sure you wouldn't tell him about the kiss, but I'd rather he not know I was at the bar at all. He wouldn't like it."

Of course he wouldn't. Big brother was a controlling jerk, and he was going to have a shit if he found out she was setting off on the adventure of living her bucket list.

"Yeah, Walter would be pissed knowing you've been at that bar every Tuesday, which, coincidentally, is the exact same day I'm always there. And the bartender says you've been doing it for a couple of months. Why is that, Chance?"

"We won't cross paths again," he continued. "You can go back to your life and I'll go back to mine, with Walter none the wiser."

Like hell she was going back to her boring, safe life. She

was living life to the fullest from now on, with or without Sherry. Again, her determination wavered as she lamented that her friend wasn't going to help her out.

And then it hit her—an idea so brilliant and perfect she couldn't help grinning. Talk about killing two birds with one stone. Show Chance Anderson exactly what he'd missed when he walked out of her life a decade ago while ticking off her bucket list items. Win-win.

She crossed back to the table and lowered into her seat, turning her face to him. "I won't tell Walter you've been lurking at the bar, but there's a price."

Chapter Five

"I need the rest of the week off." Chance lifted his chin and waited.

His big brother Michael pulled his attention from his computer screen, narrowed his eyes, and leveled his gaze on Chance from across the vast, polished mahogany desk that was once their father's before Michael took over as CEO of Anderson Enterprises.

"Absolutely not." Clearly expecting no further discussion, he returned his focus to his computer.

"Wait. No?"

Eyes still on his screen, his brother used his most practiced I'm-in-charge voice. "We're shutting down all next week. You have vacation days then."

"So, we'll close the entire office when you get married—"

"And Will. He's getting married, too."

"But I can't ask for a few days off?"

"Are *you* getting married?"

"No."

"Then, no."

He'd expected a negative reaction because of the upcoming wedding and resulting loss of office hours, and Michael always met expectations. Every. Single. Time. But he'd hoped that maybe, just this once, his brother would surprise him. He'd changed since hooking up with his fiancée, Mia, and now he even laughed at times.

Chance stared past Michael to the bright morning sunlight streaming in through the windows and engaged his nuclear option. "Then I quit."

Ha! That ranked him higher than whatever was on Michael's screen. His brother's blue eyes met his. "The fuck you say."

"The fuck I do."

"Look, Chance, I've given you vacation time for your private X Games every time you asked for it. To hike, to ski, to jump out of planes, to fucking sled across Alaska, but I'm not giving you the rest of the week off. Not when I'm closing the office for the first time since I became president."

"Hey!" Will, the middle Anderson brother, called out as he strolled into Michael's office wearing blue jeans and a T-shirt. Chance relaxed a bit. Will's good-natured, even personality was the perfect counterbalance to Michael's controlling one.

Rubbing a hand over his short military cut, a reminder of his recent Marine tours, Will looked back and forth from Chance, who stood fists at his side, to Michael, who was red in the face, still glaring from behind his computer screen, then dropped into a wing chair facing the desk. "What's going on?"

"Chance is being an idiot."

"Michael's being an asshole."

Will leaned back and grinned, flashing trademark Anderson brother dimples. "Business as usual, then." Clancy, Michael's little Shih Tzu, climbed out from his favorite spot under his master's desk and launched into Will's lap.

"Did Claire get with Mia on the flowers?" Michael asked as if Chance hadn't just pushed the red self-destruct button. "Mia was supposed to coordinate with Claire as to when to pick them up to bring them to the island."

"Dunno," Will answered, fiddling with the blue bow in the dog's hair. "I'm just trying to stay out of the way."

"So food... The chef is coming the day before to begin prep work."

For a moment, Chance thought they were just yanking his chain, but then he realized these two were honestly doing wedding planner shit. He shook his head to clear it, like a bad dream, but still, they jabbered about guests and cakes and... *Holy fuck*, the world was going mad.

His brothers were geeking out over a wedding, and his high school friend's little sister was hell-bent on a harebrained suicide mission.

Bucket list. Who on earth made bucket lists?

Genny did. And she wouldn't let him see it. He had to agree blind... He almost laughed at the irony. She had him by the balls. If he didn't help her do whatever ridiculous things were on that list, she'd tell Walter he'd been following her... and worse, maybe let slip he'd laid his hands on her. God. Walter would kill him. Genny was to be protected at all costs—and he was going to pay the price...again. All because he couldn't stay away. He'd never been able to stay away. She was like a drug. He needed more. He always had. He was addicted, but had been able to control it and hide it... Until last night when she'd kissed him. He'd fallen off the wagon. Hell, the whole fucking wagon had fallen off a cliff with him on it. One taste of Genny and he was gone. The next week would be hell.

He looked back and forth between his brothers, who were completely engrossed in an animated discussion of a tent for the reception, and shook his head. *Hopeless.* The entire world made no sense and was getting worse by the second.

Shit.

Before he could make the door, the wedding planning paused. "Where are you going?" Michael asked.

"To box up my office." Of course he wasn't really quitting, but he needed an okay from Michael, and he'd get it any way he could. Even by bluffing. His triple whammy of contract lawyer mixed with appraisal expert on top of his ability to put up with Michael's bullshit made him irreplaceable, and all three of them knew it.

"Wait. What?" Well, he'd gotten Will's attention anyway.

He shrugged nonchalantly. "Big bro wouldn't give me the rest of the week off, so I'm out of here. It's been real. Later, guys." He extended his thumb and pinkie to flash a hang-loose sign.

Faster than seemed possible, Will blocked his way from the office, dog cradled against his chest. All that military training made his brother formidable. Even with Chance's decade of martial arts training, Will gave him pause. "Hold up. Let's talk about this."

"I tried, but flowers and cakes were more important."

Will shifted his hold on the dog and gestured to the chair facing Michael's desk. "Nothing's more important than family. Talk." His brother's sincere expression made him feel like a prick. The bluff of quitting was low, but he'd get time off one way or another, and asking permission from his big brother was irksome.

He took a deep, relaxing breath and slumped down into one of the wing chairs facing the desk. How many times had he sat here in his life? Thousands. Tens of thousands, maybe. He used to make paper airplanes here while his dad mentored Michael on the business. And his dad had chosen his successor well. His oldest brother had taken Anderson

Enterprises to the top, especially the pet branch of the business, Anderson Auctions, which was world-renowned for its acquisition, representation, and placement of rare antiquities in private collections and museums.

Chance loved it here. Being the in-house counsel for Anderson Auctions fueled his fascination with history and put his law degree to good use. And he loved his brothers, even when they were jackasses, like Michael was now—and succeeded in being most of the time. What used to amount to idol worship had grown into a mutual respect. He'd never leave.

Michael might be a workaholic, but Chance wasn't, and neither was Will, who was drumming his fingers on the arm of his own chair, waiting for an explanation while Michael organized the items on his desk to be perfectly in line with the ninety-degree angles of polished mahogany surface.

"I have to take some time off. It's not optional. All documents for this week's transactions are complete and in the system. I'll have my phone. You don't need me here."

Michael paused his desk tidying and leaned back in his leather chair. "Why? Have you found some uncharted mountain pass to ski down? Or maybe you're heading to Hawaii to hang glide again. Forget it, little brother. You can break your neck *after* the wedding."

The back of Chance's scalp prickled. Ordinarily, he could maintain his calm in any circumstance. Why not now? *Genny. That's why.* She got to him every time. She always had. He'd taken punches for her. Gotten stitches for her. Even gone to jail for her... And she didn't even know.

"I have some personal business."

"What personal business?"

His muscles tightened, and it took all he had not to shoot to his feet. He was a private person, and this bordered on over-sharing. "I need to help a friend out."

"I didn't think you had any," Will kidded.

"Who?" ever-direct Michael asked.

"None of your fucking business." Well, that came out far harsher than intended.

To his surprise, Michael shut his laptop. "I'm not asking as your boss, I'm asking as your brother. The same brother you called in the past for help. You're acting odd. Are you in trouble?"

He held his breath. This was a rare side of his brother. A side he hadn't seen in a decade or so. "No." Unless being thrown together with his greatest temptation was trouble. "It's nothing like that. I'm not in trouble, and neither is she." Not if he could help it...which was why he needed the week off. Genny on her own with a bucket list had trouble written all over it, especially if the kiss last night was any indication of the rest of the list. No way was he unleashing her on the unsuspecting world.

His brothers exchanged glances. "She?" Will's eyebrows rose, and Michael grinned.

Fucking gossipy hens. Both of them.

"Just a friend."

"Who?" his brothers asked in unison.

Would the inquisition never end? He groaned in frustration. "Genny Richards. I'm going to help her with some tasks. Personal things. Totally legal and okay."

"She's that little blind girl. Walter's sister, right?"

She was far from a little girl, and Michael's "blind" descriptor caused his fists to curl. She was so much more than that. More than they'd ever understand.

"I'm playing racquetball with Walter tomorrow," Will said.

Chance's stomach dropped. "With Walter?"

"His dad talked to our dad, and well, you know how that goes, so his law firm is representing one of our smaller interests in a security installation deal. We meet up for racquetball every other week to talk about it."

Fuck, fuck, fuck. "You can't tell him about this."

Another glance between his brothers. He wasn't sure if they were surprised, amused, or both. Whatever they were, it pissed him off. He closed his eyes and centered his mood. "I'm serious. He can't know I'm helping his sister."

As if rehearsed, both brothers arched one eyebrow.

Heart racing, his desperation bordered on panic. "I never ask anything of you guys, but I'm asking now. Keep this among us."

Michael leaned forward and folded his arms on his desk. "On one condition."

Oh, shit. The consummate negotiator, always. "What?"

"You tell us everything. Now."

Surely not. He looked at Will for backup. His brother simply shrugged and said, "He's the boss."

Chapter Six

Chance paced outside Genny's building the following morning conjuring the nerve to ring the buzzer. Her apartment was on the second floor, but he still blamed the stairs for the fact he was out of breath when she opened the door.

Without a word, she took a deep inhale through her nose and gestured for him to enter. Her hair wasn't bound in its usual ponytail and flowed over her shoulders in a shiny mahogany sheet—one silky ribbon of it traveling over an intriguing expanse of bare skin down into her ample cleavage. He wondered if she knew how hot she looked in that tight, low-cut top.

"Don't just stand there ogling. Come inside. You're late."

Yep. She knew.

"Sit," she ordered, pointing to the couch closest to the door.

He crossed, instead, to the opposite side of the sparsely furnished room and sat in a chair.

She tilted her head and smiled, causing his gut to tighten. God, he'd missed her. Ten years shrank to mere days when she smiled.

"Good to know you haven't completely gone soft. I thought you'd been replaced by a lapdog," she said.

There was absolutely nothing soft about him. Between the tight red shirt and jeans that hugged her ample curves, and that smile he remembered as clearly as if he'd seen it every day of his life, he was hard as a rock. But she was off-limits, regardless of his dick's opinion. He was bad for Genny. He always had been.

While Walter and his parents were trying to keep her safe, Chance taught her how to ice skate and dive off the swim platform of the family yacht, and took her sledding. He'd loved hearing her laugh and watching her expression ignite and transform from the adrenaline spike. But that horrible night in the harbor brought home what he'd suspected in his gut all along: their friendship was dangerous for her. She'd be better off without him around. And as painful as the promise was, he'd sworn not only to Walter ten years ago, but to himself, he'd stay away from her. Well, due to the current turn of events, he certainly couldn't stay away, but he would keep the other half of the promise. "How many items are on your bucket list?"

She lowered herself into a chair across from him. "Not many."

"How many?"

An eyebrow arched. "Wouldn't you like to know?"

He stood. "I *will* know, or I'm gone."

"Oooh. So forceful. I like it."

He sat back down. "How many?"

"Ten, but one has been completed and you only need concern yourself with eight of the remaining nine. The last one I've got on my own."

He breathed a sigh of relief and scanned the room. There were pictures on the walls, black-and-whites of the city, all perfectly straight and even, which made him wonder who had helped her move in. His chest ached as he wondered who had replaced him as the go-to friend after the incident at the harbor. Maybe the woman from the bar with the spiky black hair and tight skirt—Sherry or Cherry or something.

Genny sat quietly with her face turned toward him, listening in that way she had that made it seem like she knew everything he was thinking. Maybe she did.

He had feared her bucket list items would number in the hundreds. Only ten, thank goodness. "The first item on your list was kissing me, I assume."

"Don't flatter yourself. The first one was kissing a *stranger*, which you are."

"Genny…"

"Gen," she corrected.

Okay. He'd hurt her all those years ago and she was still mad. She had every right to be. "Gen."

Shoulders square, she flipped her hair, and it cascaded over her shoulder like silky chocolate. "Before we begin, there are ground rules."

"You've done some thinking about this."

Leaning back in the plush upholstered chair, she crossed her arms over her chest protectively. "It's a ten-year-old list, buddy. You bet I've thought about it." She notched up her chin and took a breath, then held up a finger, clearly preparing to recite a rehearsed spiel. "First, you will give me complete freedom. No overprotective guardian BS. I'd have asked my brother to help me if I wanted that kind of nonsense."

"Agreed." Though he knew he couldn't curb his desire to keep her safe. He'd almost caused her death once. Never would he allow her to be harmed again on his watch.

Another finger joined the first. "Second. We will not ever talk about the past and will treat this as if we recently met and you are my assistant."

No talking about the past. It was as if she were erasing how close they'd once been—taking a jab at how much he'd missed her. He deserved this, he supposed. Walter said he'd explain why Chance had taken off, but he should have answered one of her calls or texts, despite his promise to end all contact. She'd deserved to hear it from him. "Okay."

"Third. You cannot let people know I'm carrying out bucket list items while I'm doing them."

Weird, but, "Okay."

Seemingly satisfied, she nodded and uncrossed her arms.

Two could play at this game, though. *Lapdog my ass.* "I have some rules, too."

"Lay it out, then."

"With regard to your first rule: I'll allow nothing that will bring you harm. I'll follow your lead, but we're doing it my way if I deem it safer."

She frowned, but nodded agreement.

"Second. I'll respect your wish to not talk about the past with the caveat that I believe it's a mistake. But in return, I need complete honesty from you. If I'm to risk losing my longtime friend for this escapade, I need things straightforward. You must keep promises and do what you say you're going to do."

"I've never lied or broken a promise to you."

"Nuh-uh. No talking about the past. Your rule." And she *had* broken a promise—the promise to sit still on that dock and wait. He couldn't go through something like that again.

"And third." *And most important.* "Never touch me."

Her mouth dropped open, then snapped shut in a grimace. "News flash. I'm blind. I might need some assistance that requires touching to navigate safely."

"Assistance is one thing. Tell me and I'll help you, but warn me first. And don't touch me if you can help it."

A flicker of hurt crossed her face, but disappeared as quickly as it came. "Fine. No touching you. And the same goes for me. Hands off."

"That goes without saying."

"Fine."

"Fine."

After a moment of silence, she snickered, then giggled. By the time she hit a full-out laugh, he'd joined her. "We sound like a couple of bratty teenagers," she said.

"Reverting to old ways, I suppose." He stood and tore his eyes away from her. God, she was pretty. This week was going to be his private version of heaven and hell all rolled together. "What's first on the list?"

"Roller coaster."

"No more kissing, then?"

The side of her mouth quirked up. "No. Kissing on a roller coaster seems like a tooth breaker to me. I only specified riding the Cyclone."

That seemed simple and safe enough. "That shouldn't take long. What's after that?"

"Skydiving."

So much for simple and safe. "And after that?"

She crossed to the door and snatched her cane and jacket from the coatrack. "That should be enough for today, don't you think?"

More than enough.

Chapter Seven

They reached Coney Island before lunchtime, which suited Gen because despite her bravado, she was nervous and better off on an empty stomach. She'd always wanted to ride a roller coaster, but her family thought the pressure on her eyes would be bad for her, which she found comical. How much blinder could completely blind be?

They'd arrived by private car, and the cold air seemed like an all-out assault after the cozy limo interior. One of the perks of hanging out with Chance Anderson: limousine rides. She'd loved it when she was younger and loved it now. He even had the same driver—the one with the slight British accent named Jacob, who always used her full name and made her feel like a princess.

The cool March wind blowing off the water didn't dampen the thrill, though. Exciting sounds of carnival music and laughter mixed with the smells of burned sugar and salt air. As they neared the Cyclone, the rattling and rumble of the large wooden coaster thundered in her chest, and the squeals of riders launched her adrenaline into her head and fingertips.

"Nervous?" Chance asked from beside her as they moved closer to the ride.

"Never," she said with as much bravado as possible. Scared stiff was more like it, but that was normal, or so she'd been told by Sherry, who should have been here with her instead of her childhood heartbreak.

"This way," he said from several feet in front of her. Her cane tripped along a wooden walkway until it transitioned into concrete. "We're in line now," he said. "Because it's still the off season, it won't be a long wait."

She nodded, too anxious to speak. The rational side of her knew there was nothing to fear. This roller coaster had been in operation since the late 1920s and had been refurbished loads of times, including recently. The irrational side of her was freaking completely out.

"I read somewhere it reaches sixty miles an hour on one of the big drops," Chance said from right behind her. *Wait.* He was in front of her a moment ago. Usually, she had a great sense of her surroundings. Must have been the anxiety over the ride.

"Yeah, I read that, too. How much longer?" The wait was killing her. So was being this near Chance. She could smell him—that clean smell she now associated with him. She was curious what he looked like and what he was wearing, but thanks to the hands-off rule, she'd probably never know. He had on something with some texture, though, because there was a *shooshing* sound when he moved. Maybe a windbreaker.

"What color are you wearing?" she asked, as much from nervous energy as curiosity.

"Brown jacket and blue jeans. Red-and-black striped sweater."

"Earth, eyes, blood, and night."

"It used to be 'sky' for blue," he remarked.

It had been a slip. Sherry had told her he had beautiful blue eyes last night, and it stuck as her color reference. She'd been born blind and had never seen colors, but she liked to associate them with moods and other objects. Color was theoretical in her mind, but it helped to be able to relate to sighted people if she formed concrete associations.

She felt the heat from him directly behind her, and she fought the urge to lean back. When they were younger, she'd have never thought twice about leaning against him. They had constantly been in contact—not in a sexual way. Just in a familiar way. It had grounded her in strange locations.

She'd missed him, and even with him this close, loneliness pounded through her like the sounds of the ride overhead.

"My brother has blue eyes is why I changed it." She sensed him stiffen at her jab. "Have you done this before? Ridden on the Cyclone?" she asked.

"Yes. Many times."

Only to him, this was probably nothing. He did things that didn't come with seat belts and safety padding. Things she could hardly imagine having the nerve to do.

The people on the ride screamed in unison and she shuddered. "What do you see?"

"The structure is wood painted white," he said in a soothing tone, "with red and yellow accents. The cars themselves are red and seat eight people in four pairs. There's lots of padding and a lap restraint. Very safe."

"You'll ride with me, right?" Her voice sounded odd and breathy—needy, which she hated.

"If you want me to."

"Yes," she answered faster than intended.

A loud hydraulic hiss and staccato squeals from brakes sounded directly in front of her.

"We're up," he said quietly, lips near enough to her ear for his breath to send chills down her spine. "Do you want me in first or last?"

"First. I need help. You'll have to touch me."

"An attendant is waiting to help you."

"No. You. Only you," she blurted.

Chance flinched at her words. Words he'd dreamed at night when his guard was completely down and his heart took over in his sleep. His guard was not down now—just the opposite. Everything in him was on hyperalert as he squeezed her hand and guided her to the landing. Being around her had always had this effect on him. Colors seemed brighter and noises louder, like her mere presence fed his adrenaline addiction. The attendant stood nearby and took the cane when he relieved her of it.

"I'm right here." He stepped into the car and grabbed both of her hands, then described the configuration and gently guided her into the seat next to him, careful not to pull or yank her, but to let her use him for balance as she found her own way. The attendant might have rushed her into the car. He'd learned long ago that she became disoriented when pulled or pushed. He'd always admired her for being at her best when taking on new things at her own pace.

Finally settled, she turned her face to him and grinned, sending all concern and worry he'd had packing.

"Arms up," the attendant ordered and they both raised their arms as the lap restraint was engaged. Still, she grinned as the brakes made a hiss and the car lurched forward, then jerked and began rolling for real.

She clutched the bar in front of her. "This is super hard with no vision. I can't anticipate anything, so it's pretty intense."

"Well, it's going to climb for a while, and then the first

drop ends in a rise and a sharp left before another drop."

She nodded.

"Do you want me to narrate?"

"No. I want to experience it as it comes with no warnings. Maybe not knowing is more fun."

Maybe it was. "Okay, I'll close my eyes and we'll do this together."

"No peeking," she said as the car tilted and began to clatter up the incline.

"I won't peek if you don't," he teased as they reached the top and the car paused momentarily.

Her laughter rang in his ears as the g-forces hit. Taking the ride with his eyes closed was unlike anything he'd done before. He couldn't relax even for a second, not knowing which way he'd be pitched next. He had to remain tight and at the ready at all times for whatever came at him. Much like Genny had lived her entire life—tensing for what would come at her next out of nowhere.

The no-touching rule was abandoned on the first turn when she slid into him, still giggling and squealing. Then he was leaning into her as the car shifted direction and went up for another drop.

He couldn't help peeking as the car slowed at the top of a rise. She'd closed her eyes, probably because of the wind, and a huge grin was plastered on her face. And for the first time he realized it wasn't the accident that had made him so protective and fond, it was the woman herself—or girl at one time. She was amazing.

"I can feel you looking at me," she said. "You're cheati—aaaaaaaaaaah!" she squealed as the car plummeted down another fall.

More exciting than taking the ride with his eyes closed was taking it watching *her*. Expressive, beautiful, and alive, she was better than anything he'd experienced in recent years. God, he'd missed her.

As the ride ended and they screeched to a halt, she was still laughing, free of all pretense and layers. And he found himself in awe.

Chance Anderson knew at that moment, he was completely and totally screwed. No way would he make the week without breaking every one of his own rules.

Bundled back into the limo with Nathan's hot dogs and cheese fries, Gen was certain she'd reached the high point of her life to date. Side by side, she and Chance feasted from the same tray as if there had never been a rift or a decade of separation between them.

It struck her as odd that they could fall back into such familiarity after so long a time. Eerie almost. "You're breath's going to stink after this," she teased. "Onions and relish. Ew."

"Good thing I'm not kissing you after all that chili and cheese," he said, wiping something from her chin with his thumb. "Chili. Yum."

"Did you just lick that off your finger?"

"You bet I did. Want to trade?"

"No way. Onions. Yuck."

"I figured you'd outgrown your dislike of onions by now."

She froze and gave herself a mental shake. She'd promised herself, when she decided to ask Chance to help her, that she'd guard her heart this time. She needed to be careful. He'd taken off without a word before, and he was likely to do it again. She took another bite of hot dog, schooling her face into a neutral expression.

She hadn't outgrown her dislike of onions, nor had she outgrown her distrust of Chance.

"So. Skydiving. I have a line on that. Want to knock that

one out now, or have you had enough excitement for today?

"Let's do it today." The sooner this ended, the better. She hadn't anticipated him knotting her all up inside again. She'd thought to show him how self-sufficient she was as an adult, then cut him loose without a backward glance. So far, not so good. "Never enough excitement."

He pulled out his phone and texted someone, then gave the driver, Jacob, an address in New Jersey.

"That's kind of far," she said, pulling out her own phone. "There are airports a lot closer than that. Sherry said a man she dated jumped with some guys who take off out of Islip."

"This is better than that. I know a lot about skydiving, and this is perfect."

Sticking in her earbuds, she typed the address he'd given the driver into her phone. "Sky Bird Adventure Vertical Wind Tunnel," the phone recited. "Indoor skydiving for all body types and experience levels."

She yanked out her earbuds and turned to face him. "Are you shitting me? It's a wind tunnel. No plane? No jump? No deal."

"I will remind you now of rule number one: I'll allow nothing that will bring you harm. I'll follow your lead, but we're doing it my way if I deem it safer." Fabric slid across leather as he shifted in the seat. "Skydiving is reckless and dangerous in this case. I deem this a safer alternative."

"But you've done it. A *lot*. You even did it back in high school."

"Yes, I did."

"Why can't I?"

He shifted in his seat again. Good, she'd made him uncomfortable.

"Again. This is better. It simulates skydiving without the fear of equipment or user failure. It lets you fly much longer than an actual jump. Yes. I've jumped out of a plane, but I've done this, too, and I think you'll like it much better."

She crossed her arms over her chest and huffed. "No way. No plane, no jump, no deal."

"Genny."

"Gen!"

"Gen." He took her face in his hands.

"No touching. Your rule."

"Fuck my rule and listen to me. I can't let you jump out of a plane. Just because I've done it doesn't mean it's right for you. You might not be scared, but I am. You almost died because of me once." His voice broke as he spoke, which caused a painful twinge in her chest.

"No talking about the past. My rule," she admonished.

"Fuck *your* rule, too."

And at that she smiled. She could almost hear his smile back, but to be sure, she touched his face. They remained like that for a moment, holding each other's faces over a tray of half-eaten hot dogs.

"I bet we look pretty stupid, Anderson."

"Good thing you can't see, Richards."

When his hands moved down her face to her jawline, her entire body thrummed to life like it had in the bar when he touched her. He swept his fingers down her neck and across her shoulders, then dropped his hands and leaned back. "I'm firm on this, Gen. I can't let you jump from a plane. If you don't like it, find another 'assistant.'"

She gave a calculated, long-suffering sigh. "Wind tunnel it is."

He shifted the tray from between them. "You done?"

"Yep."

"Good. I want the rest of your chili dog."

"That's probably not a good idea before you do this flight simulator thing."

"Mmm. Mmm," he mumbled, mouth full. "Not *my*

bucket list. You're on your own this time. I'm waiting in the car. You don't need me for this."

For a moment, she was startled, then angry, and then, just like that, she was pleased. He was giving her the opportunity to do this odd, adventurous thing on her own. To prove not only to him, but to herself she was capable and could do this without assistance. Damn right she could.

"So that knocks three of ten, leaving seven."

"Six. I don't need your help with the last one."

"What is it?"

"None of your business, like I told you before."

"What's next, then?"

"Skinny-dipping!" She grinned. "Remember that pool we used to go to in the summer? We're going to break into it at midnight.."

"Ha!" he barked. "When did you make this list?"

Before you broke my heart. "When I was fifteen."

"Baby, that pool's been a parking lot for five years."

The sound of the pavement under the limo tires changed as they crossed a bridge. She leaned back against the soft leather seat and closed her eyes, imagining the pool from her childhood. She'd loved the feel of floating and the way sound was muffled when her ears were barely underwater. Her favorite memories from the pool were jumping off the diving board hand in hand with Chance and playing Marco Polo with him for hours on end. "Well, I've got to do something to replace it, then, or I won't get my wish."

"What wish?"

"Don't you know anything about bucket lists? If you complete everything on it with the original list still intact, you get a wish."

"Ah. Well, let me think on it. I'll find an appropriate substitute." The napkin crinkled as he wiped his mouth and hands. She remembered how he'd caught the chili from her chin with his thumb and licked it off, and she imagined herself licking the chili from his face and fingers. Licking his entire body. Licking his... *Stop!* Where on earth did that come from?

It had to be the residual adrenaline from the roller coaster ride or maybe her anticipation of her upcoming fake skydive giving her crazy imaginings. Whatever it was, thoughts like that were taboo and needed to stay relegated to the privacy of her bedroom. The one place she couldn't inadvertently send the wrong signal and end up in a heap of trouble with an irreparably shattered heart.

Before long, they came to a stop, and Chance handed over her cane. "The owner is a friend of Michael's, my oldest brother, so you'll get the star treatment. They're expecting you. Door is thirty or so feet at ten o'clock. Go fly, Gen. Soar."

Chapter Eight

Chance had never experienced an hour this long. Even the night he'd been arrested seemed shorter than this. Maybe because he had dreaded seeing Genny after his night in jail, and he couldn't wait to see her now. He checked his watch for the hundredth time and resisted texting Michael's friend to check up on how she was doing. She was a grown woman and only required assistance, not a babysitter. Not that he'd ever considered himself her babysitter. They'd been friends. Best friends.

Well, not anymore. She'd made it more than clear that their past meant nothing to her.

"I'll be driving Mr. William and Miss Claire to the airport in the morning, and then after that, your oldest brother needs the car to take Miss Mia to her wedding dress fitting," Jacob said from the driver's seat.

Chance shook his head. "I never thought I'd see the day Michael got married."

"He says the same about you, sir."

That was surprising. "He does?"

"It concerns him that you don't date."

Wow. So much for shy, impersonal Jacob. He'd known the guy forever, and he was never one to be direct.

"How do you feel about that, Jacob?"

"I believe you are discerning, sir."

What the hell did that mean? This guy had driven him around since he was in grade school. "How so?"

"I believe you are the type of man who waits for exactly what he wants and is not satisfied to make do with substitutes while he waits."

He was speaking in code or some such nonsense. He sat back and stared at the strip of Jacob's face visible in the rearview mirror. Not one to beat around the bush, Chance pushed further. "What am I waiting on?"

Jacob's eyes flickered to the left, and he nodded to something outside. "Her."

Chance followed his gaze, and his heart thumped wildly as Genny emerged from the building, face alight. Yes. It had always been her.

His gaze met Jacob's brown eyes in the mirror. Was he that transparent? "Have you talked to my brothers about this?"

"No. My limo is like Las Vegas. What happens in Vegas—"

"—stays in Vegas. Yes, yes, I know. I'd like you to stick to that policy, please. She's not like-minded."

"You're wrong," he said. "She's discerning, too. And she's ten steps ahead of you. She always has been." And with that, he got out to open her door. "This way, Miss Genevieve."

Chance closed his eyes, memories playing through his mind like a slide show. Yes. Jacob had driven them around all the time, Genny, Walter, and him. To movies, to school, even to toilet paper friends' houses. That was over a decade ago. He opened his eyes and watched as Jacob guided Gen into the car. A woman who was familiar, yet at the same time, a complete stranger. The woman he'd been told was ten steps ahead of him.

"That was awesome!" she said, plopping down in the facing seat, dropping the cane on the floor. Her hair was a tangled mess and her cheeks pink—a maddeningly attractive combination. "You should have done it with me." She made a futile attempt to finger-comb her hair. "Is there still some Coke left?"

He passed her what was left of his drink from Nathan's.

"Oh my God, that was perfect. You were so right. It beat the heck out of jumping out of a plane." She took a large sip. "There was this huge fan under this net thing and I had to wear goggles and a helmet and what felt like a space suit. The guy said I looked great. Nothing says sexy like a space suit, right?"

"Space suits are my go-to for sexy for sure." He shifted in his seat, wishing he'd witnessed her skydiving. "I prefer scuba gear, though. You'd rock skintight neoprene, and those flippers drive guys wild."

"You had me at skintight," she said. "I'm all about being able to feel the landscape." She ran her hands up her belly to her ribs, stopping under her breasts, which were perfectly displayed in her tight shirt. "The valleys and especially the hills. Maybe we should add a scuba dive to the list."

Holy shit. Jacob was right. This was more than just friendly banter. The undercurrent was real and mature and... *damn.* He met the driver's amused gaze in the mirror. Walter would kill him for the thoughts going through his mind right then.

"Where to, sir?"

Chance shook his head to clear it. "Um, where next, Gen?"

"Columbus Circle. Do you have a change of clothes?"

That didn't sound good. "No."

"Mr. Michael leaves a bag with several changes in the trunk. His clothes should fit you. Miss Mia has a bag in there as well."

"Why do they have clothes in the trunk?" Chance wondered aloud.

Jacob's only reply was an arch of an eyebrow.

He waved a hand dismissively. "Never mind. Vegas. I get it. You heard the lady. Columbus Circle."

Still buzzing from skydiving, Gen had trouble keeping her hands to herself. All this adrenaline made her horny; that and her nearness to Chance was a dangerous combo. Maybe this is why he'd always done crazy things. At least he was all the way on the other side of the limo. She could feel him watching her, though, and the thought of his checking her out made her nipples tighten and her lower body heat. Maybe she should have asked him to leave the privacy divider between the driver and the cabin open so that they weren't so…alone.

"What are we doing at Columbus Circle? I thought breaking into the pool at midnight was next." His voice was low and rumbly and sexy as hell. Her plan had completely backfired. Instead of showing him what he was missing, he tortured her with what she'd never have. All thanks to her overprotective big brother and Chance's misplaced sense of honor or whatnot.

"I skipped that, because it's something I can do on my own, like number ten." She shrugged and forced herself to relax against the leather seat to hide the fact that she was wound up as tight as a spring. "I put this back into the schedule because we have time and it's on the way back to my apartment."

"Exactly what are we doing there?"

"Running through the fountain, of course. No good bucket list is complete without a run through a public fountain."

"But of course. How silly of me."

She heard amusement in his voice and hoped the chilled water of the fountain might cool some of the sexual tension bouncing around the limousine like Ping-Pong balls. Then, a horrible thought hit her.

"Oh, no. We can't do this. Well, *you* can't do this."

"Because?"

"You're an Anderson. You'll make the tabloids or something. I read about your brothers all the time."

"Ah. But you're overlooking two important points. First, I have no intention of running through the fountain. It's your list to complete. I'm just here to facilitate your success. Second, I'm the invisible Anderson brother. There is nothing high-profile about me. I don't do charity balls, or make power deals, or date supermodels like Michael did before Mia. I'm not a homegrown hero with a socialite past like Will. I'm just the little brother nobody notices."

"God. That sounds pathetic."

He laughed. "It's deliberate. I hate that kind of attention. If you want to run through a fountain, I'm happy to go with you. I just wish you had chosen to do this in a month, after it warms up some."

"Inconvenient, but most things worth doing are."

He fell quiet for a moment, and she itched to touch his face to read his expression. When they were teens, she kept her fingers on his face so that she could "see" him as he spoke. Touching him now would be a disaster, though. Her fifteen-year-old crush didn't hold a candle to the adult lust threatening to spontaneously combust inside her now.

"Out of an abundance of caution," he said, "we should

get out a block or more away. Even though I slide under the radar, the limo might draw attention, and a hot woman running through a frigid fountain is certainly noteworthy." He pushed the intercom button. "Let's do a drop-off at Lincoln Center instead, please, Jacob."

Hot woman. Every cell in her body heated with delight. That's not something he'd say to someone he still saw as a little girl.

By the time they'd walked the short distance from Lincoln Center to Columbus Circle, Gen was having second thoughts. At fifteen, running through this fountain seemed like such a cool thing to do. At twenty-five, it felt ridiculous.

They crossed the street and entered the circle. "What do you see?" she asked.

"A statue of Christopher Columbus surrounded by a concrete area ringed by a shallow, circular fountain with jets, divided in thirds by walkways. All in all, I see a disaster waiting for you to come along."

She laughed. "No. I mean people and obstacles."

"Woman reading on bench at nine o'clock, cops on other side of street bordering the southwest corner of Central Park at two o'clock, and tourists passing through the circle all over the clock. Good luck." He ushered her to a bench, and she sat.

"Have you ever done this before?"

"Never. And I don't plan to."

She sat and removed a calf-high boot. "This is a stupid idea, isn't it?"

"Some of the better things in my life have started out as bad ideas."

Off came the other boot and then her socks. "Like what?" She lowered her bare feet to the cold concrete and gasped.

"Like helping you with this bucket list business."

She stilled, letting his words tumble over and over in her

head. This was one of the better things in his life. Being here. With *her*.

She reached toward him and made contact. Unfortunately, the thing she brushed across felt suspiciously like the zipper fly of his jeans. He hissed through his teeth and took a quick step back.

Yep. Nailed it. "Sorry."

She patted the bench next to her, toes curling from the cold. The air moved, and his jacket made the swooshing sound again as he complied. Careful to keep her hands high this time, she felt her way up his arm, over his shoulder, and took his face in her hands, pulling him closer. "The no-touching rule sucks," she said, not even embarrassed at the husky sound of her voice.

"Agreed." His breaths came in heated puffs against her skin.

She ran her fingertips over his warm, smooth bottom lip. "I say we ditch that rule completely."

"You'll get no objection from me."

The moment in the limo earlier, sharing hot dogs while still high from the roller coaster adrenaline, didn't even come close to this. *This* new high point in her life. They were right on the precipice. Lips almost touching, breaths mingling in the electric tension strung between them. She took a shuddering breath, enjoying the heady buzz of balancing on that razor's edge.

"Kiss me, Gen."

She hovered a breath away, entire body humming, and didn't move.

He closed the distance, but this kiss was way different than the encounter in the bar. No slow exploration or warm-up. He thrust his fingers into her hair, tilted her head, and took her mouth with a hunger that rivaled her own. Hot, insistent, purposeful. No gentle caress. Nothing in reserve.

This was a get-a-room kind of kiss and it made her toes curl—and not from the cold this time.

He broke away with a groan and rested his forehead against hers, breaths coming in heavy gasps.

Slowly, the world sharpened into focus around her: a car honk, unknown footsteps traversing the circle, a siren in the distance, indistinguishable voices of passersby, the rumble and rattle of cars and trucks on the street as they made their way around the fountain. Somewhere across the street, a policeman blew a whistle in the park.

Chance disentangled his fingers from her hair and straightened next to her on the bench. "You'd better go run through that fountain before we get arrested for public indecency," he said, still out of breath. "Because one more second like that, and some clothes will be joining your boots on the pavement."

She laughed.

"Seriously."

"What do you see?"

"Nothing but you."

"I'm not kidding."

"Neither am I." He ran his thumb over her bottom lip. "What do I see? Your lips are pink and swollen from kissing me." He grazed his knuckles over her cheekbone. "Your color is high with excitement. Your hair is all a mess because I held on for dear life so I wouldn't grope you in public." He kissed the tip of her nose. "Your nose is red because it's chilly." He stood and pulled her to her feet. "Now, go run your cute ass through that fountain so I can get you back home, where you're no longer exposed to the cold or to me."

Chapter Nine

He should never have kissed her. *Never, never, never.* Chance paced the length of his bedroom and back again. What had he been thinking? Nothing. That's when he always got in trouble. When he stopped thinking and felt instead.

"Dammit!" he shouted after another lap of the room. He should have known by now that indulging addiction was reckless and never ended well. And he was as addicted to Gen as he was to adrenaline. He'd accepted that fact while waiting in the car outside the indoor skydiving venue for her. Even the family chauffeur knew.

Not accepting her invitation to come up to her apartment when they'd dropped her off had been the hardest thing he'd done in a long time. Wet from head to toe and wrapped up in his jacket, she looked delicious. He'd imagined all manner of ways to warm her up, none of them in accordance with her big brother's wishes. But in the end, he'd done the right thing and sent her up alone.

And here he was, pacing his apartment with a perpetual boner, shaking and cursing like he was going through DTs.

Well, he *was* detoxing, in a manner. He was coming down off a Genny high, which was more potent than any adventure he'd been on or anything he'd experimented with in college.

Walter would be so pissed if he ever found out.

He'd just have to see that he never found out and make sure it never happened again. That was the only solution. Quit cold turkey. That was the most efficient and effective solution. *Efficient and effective.* God. He sounded like his brother Michael.

He couldn't just go back on his word completely, though. He'd make good on his promise to take her skinny-dipping, but then he was done. He'd assist her the same way he had with skydiving. He'd make sure she was safe and let her do it on her own.

He groaned and adjusted his still-raging erection as he imagined joining her naked in the cold water. *No.* There was no way in hell he was going to get naked anywhere near her. Today at the fountain was evidence enough he was in way over his head. She deserved better than the brief touch-and-go he could offer. As Walter had made clear ten years ago, she needed someone who would keep her out of trouble, not lead her headfirst into unsafe situations, like Chance had done so many times until it backfired and nearly killed her at the harbor.

A knock on his door pulled him back to the present.

It was later than his brothers ever came by. He cracked the door to find Gen grinning. *Shit.* "How'd you find my place?"

The smile dropped from her face, probably from his less-than-welcoming greeting. "I called your office and spoke with your secretary, who remembered me from when we were kids. She put me in touch with Jacob, who seemed more than happy to drop me off."

Of course Jacob was. He looked over his shoulder at his

disaster of an apartment and shook his head. Maybe seeing what a slob he was would convince her he wasn't worth the effort. But she couldn't see. Hell, even his *place* was dangerous to her. Obstacles everywhere, as opposed to her tidy, sparsely furnished home.

"Come on in, but do so at your own risk. There's stuff all over the floor. I never have guests."

He guided her to the head of the dining table, deftly avoiding a gym bag.

"What's on the floor?"

"Workout equipment, mainly, and some weapons. I was in a hurry yesterday after I got back from the dojang." She tilted her head that way she did when she wanted more information. "I've been doing tae kwon do for almost ten years." He shoved the gym bag under a chair with his foot.

She nodded. "Walter mentioned that."

He picked up his shin guards and pitched them into the bag. "It helps me stay focused. It...takes the edge off."

"The edge off of what?" Again she tilted her head, but he didn't oblige. He'd already revealed too much. Instead, he placed two swords in the cabinet while she turned her head to listen. "Hmmm. It sounds like you need to catch me up on your past, Chance."

He flipped the light off and lowered himself into a chair closest to her. It was easier if he couldn't see her face clearly. Now that he'd felt her passion, being near her hurt—and not just from his ever-present hard-on when she was around. It was his chest—his heart—that ached the most. Like right after he'd been forbidden to see her all those years ago. "We agreed not to mention the past."

"We also agreed to not touch, but we both know how that worked out."

"About that..."

Reaching out, she swept across the table until she found

and clutched his hand. "Don't, Chance." Her grip was strong. Just like she was. Like he wanted to be. "Please, don't."

He closed his eyes, making his experience closer to hers. "I'll help you with this next task, but I'm not so sure continuing on after that is a good idea."

"Why?" She moved her hands to his face like she did when they were children to read his expressions. He reveled in her touch.

"You know exactly why."

Gently, she brushed his closed eyelids. "Because we might kiss again?"

"Yes."

She adjusted her fingers slightly so that they spanned more of his face. "And that's a problem because…"

He pulled out of her reach and stood abruptly, the chair scraping across the hardwood floor and almost tipping over behind him. "You know why."

"No! I don't! Tell me. Explain it, Chance, because I don't have a clue why we can't be friends—why we can't be more than friends." The side of her fist came down on the table with a *thud*. He'd never heard her raise her voice before. "We're grown-up people living grown-up lives." She took a deep breath and ran her fingers through her hair. "It makes no sense at all to me, so explain it."

"I made a promise." And for Chance that meant something. All his life, he'd watched his father break promises to his mom. Had seen her hide her tears and put on a good face for her sons. He'd vowed to never be like that. "I promised your family I'd stay away from you."

"Why?" The hurt in her voice turned the air in his lungs to ice. "Why would you do something like that when we were so close? You were my best friend, Chance. My only friend. The only person who would help me do cool stuff."

He stared over her shoulder at the bag of mountain-climbing equipment on top of the cabinet housing his swords. His gaze slid over to the corner where his skis were bagged for his heli-skiing trip next month, and leaning at the ready was his favorite snowboard. To the left, his scuba gear was organized and prepped for when the whim hit—which could be any time. His body craved adrenaline. Walter was right. He loved danger and didn't appreciate its lure for Genny, and because of that, leaving had been the right thing to do. It would be the right thing to do right now.

"Because I'm bad for you." He heard Walter's voice saying it in his head as he spoke. "Your getting hurt was inevitable. I'm just relieved you didn't die."

"That's ridiculous."

"Regardless of how you feel about it, I gave him my word."

"And you gave *me* your word that you'd help me accomplish all ten items on my list."

"Nine. You said you had the last one taken care of."

"Nine. There are only five left then. Four after tonight. Why does your promise to him mean more than your promise to me?"

"It doesn't."

"Then you'll help me."

"It's a terrible idea."

"Yet earlier today, you said that it was one of the best things you'd ever done."

He took a deep breath and let it out slowly, resigning himself to keeping the promise he should never have made to her. It would have been better to confess to Walter he'd kissed his little sister and let the fists fly as they may. This was just prolonging the inevitable and probably making it worse for all of them.

Gen waited while Chance made up his mind. His behavior made no sense to her. The stupid promise was made ten years ago. Bad for her? No. What was bad for her was living her life inside safety cones, and she was sick of it. Chance wanted her. She was certain of it now, yet he pushed her away again and again.

For years, she thought it was something about her that had driven him away. Now she suspected it was something inside himself, and there was a lot more to it than a lame promise to her big brother. That kiss at the fountain was the real deal. Passion like that couldn't be faked.

Her agenda since this whole thing began had done a one-eighty. She no longer wanted to hurt him and show him what he'd missed when he left all those years ago; she wanted to make up for lost time. She wanted to kiss and touch and hold him like she had in her dreams—and in her imagination when she was alone. She wanted him to see her for the woman she had become. She wanted him to help her scratch number ten off her list, finally, after a decade of waiting.

"Okay," he said. "I'll go through with it, but I want to see the list. Keeping me in the dark is counterproductive."

"Kinda like being me, huh?"

"You know what's on the list, so, no."

He wanted to see the list. *Fine.* She'd show it to him. She pulled it out of the back of her phone case and handed it to him, waiting for his reaction with a smirk.

To her shock, he didn't ask what to make of it. Instead, she heard him running his fingers across the surface. *Shit.* He could read braille. When had that happened?

"So… Speedboat, slow dance in the rain…"

"Give it back!" She swept her arms in the direction of his voice and made contact with his chest. Grabbing his T-shirt in her fist, she reached for his right arm.

"Play spin the bottle?"

"I was fifteen! Please give it back."

She had to get it away from him before he read number ten.

"Sleep under the stars…"

That was number nine. She lunged and made a mad grab for the scrap of paper, but only managed to rip a corner off of it.

"Lose it."

Crap, crap, crap. She slumped to the floor and buried her face in her hands to hide what was surely the mother of all blushes based on the hot flush crawling over her skin.

"Lose what?"

He could not be that dense.

"Oh…*that.*" He sat down beside her, turned her hand over, and placed the list in her palm.

"I was fifteen," she said again as if it made a difference.

"I'm sorry, Gen. I didn't mean to upset you. You handed it to me."

"I didn't know you could read braille."

He tipped her chin toward him with his fingertips and wiped away an escaped tear. "You don't know a lot of things about me."

She sniffed. It was wet and gross and embarrassing. A double whammy on top of the read-aloud. He kissed her forehead, and she felt like she had when she was ten and had fallen and skinned her knee. He'd kissed her forehead then, too.

She pushed the clock function on her phone. "Ten fifty-four," it announced.

"Let's go," he said, brushing her hair out of her face. "Time for us to sneak onto some private property and skinny-dip."

She sniffled again, and didn't even try to hold back her grin. The prospect of getting naked with him certainly didn't make her feel like a ten-year-old. Not even a little bit.

Chapter Ten

Gen giggled as Chance led her by the hand. "Have you done this before?"

"Skinny-dip? Yes, many times. Not at this location, though," he whispered. "We're almost there. We just need to climb this chain-link fence, and we're in."

"Where are we?" She laid her hands flat against the cold fence and hung on while it strained and rattled as he climbed over ahead of her.

"It's a private residential lake on Long Island," he whispered, guiding her hands to the top of the short fence, no taller than four feet. "Can you climb this on your own?"

"Of course I can." As she shoved her foot in one of the wire diamonds, the gravel crunched on the drive behind them and she squeaked.

"It's okay. That's just Jacob leaving to wait at the end of the street so we aren't spotted."

She powered up to the top of the fence and straddled it, loving the feel of his warm hands steadying her by the waist as she swung her leg over. "I think it's because you don't want him to see me naked."

"That, too."

He pulled her free of the fence and held her against him until she was steady. "Pond is about fifty feet straight ahead," he whispered in her ear, sending shocks of energy through her entire body. "Are you sure you want to go through with this?"

She crept along behind him with her fingers though his belt loops, fighting back giggles. "Are you kidding? I've waited ten years to do this. Are you going to chicken out on me?"

"Never!"

"Shhhhhh."

He chuckled and stopped, causing her to bump into him full-body from behind with an *oof.*

"What the heck?" she whispered. "It's like the blind leading the blind here."

"I'm going to show you precisely how well I can see if you mash your breasts against me again." He headed off once more with her in tow.

"Well, then, warn me before you stop." A rustling came from somewhere on the right. "What was that?" she whispered, moving her grip to the belt loops nearest the front of his pants to get closer to him.

"Stopping," he said, straightening from his tiptoe crouch.

Still holding him tight, she buried her face in the back of his shirt. "There's something in the bushes or weeds to our right, and I'm scared it's going to jump out at us."

He cleared his throat. "Honey, there's something in my pants, and if you don't turn loose of where you're holding me, it might jump out at us, too."

"Oh." She giggled and released him. "Sorry. I'm kind of excited."

"Clearly, so am I."

"Are we near the water?"

He took her hand and she noticed he was trembling. "There's a small dock. We'll leave our clothes there." She followed a few more feet, and he paused. "Three steps and then a ten-by-ten or so wooden dock. Ready?"

She nodded, trusting him fully, which gave her pause for a moment. She'd vowed she'd never trust him, yet here she was, about to get naked while trespassing. She made the three steps and he steadied her again.

"You good?" he asked. "We should be quick about this. It would be hard to explain if we got caught."

There was a rustling, then the distinct sound of a zipper, then a splash followed by "Holy fuck it's cold! Hurry up!"

"Turn around," she whispered.

"Are you kidding me?"

"I can't see you, so you shouldn't be allowed to see me. Fair is fair."

"It's dark. I'm fucking freezing my balls off. Get naked and get in here, woman."

With quick movements, she kicked off her shoes, peeled off her shirt, and stripped out of her jeans, glad he'd insisted on leaving their coats in the car. Then, still wearing her panties and bra, she took several steps in the direction of his splashes. "Where's the end?" A completely unexpected panic washed over her, causing her muscles to seize momentarily. Her voice trembled as memories of the night on the dock came back. "I don't want to fall in the water."

"Oh, baby. I'm sorry. You won't fall. I'm right here." Vibrations traveled up her legs from where he patted the dock, guiding her to him. "Come to my voice and I'll stop you before you get to the edge." There was splashing and several thumps as he climbed out onto the dock. Then he wrapped her in his arms. "I'm right here. I won't let you fall."

"I'm good," she said, shivering as the water from his body

ran down hers. "Is it deep enough to jump?"

"Yes. And it has a muddy bottom."

"On three," she said, "Just like we used to do off the side of the pool."

He took her hand and they stood shivering, side by side. "One, two, three!"

"Cold" didn't even come close to describing the water. It stung all over, and she gasped for air like she had all those years ago as familiar terror struck, causing her to flail and kick.

"I've got you," he said, wrapping her in his arms and pulling her against him. "You're okay, I'm here." Her panic subsided, and after a moment, she stopped fighting the water, still shivering. "Not alone. I'm right here with you this time. I'm standing on the bottom holding you and there are no barnacles to cut you." She relaxed against him and he kissed her ear. "Okay?"

She nodded, surprised how affected she was by those memories and how quickly he calmed her. He seemed more at ease, too. Maybe it was therapeutic for him, as well. They were facing down a demon together.

"Now," he said. "While I'm cold as hell and ready to end this, I have to point out that you are technically doing it wrong."

"What?" She snuggled closer to his body for warmth.

He groaned as their skin made greater contact. "Not that. You're doing that just right, but this." He snapped her bra against her back. "You're technically not skinny-dipping. You have on the equivalent of a swimsuit." With one deft movement, he unhooked the clasp in the front, slid the strap off one shoulder and then the other. A tightening of his muscles was followed by a wet *thwack,* most certainly the result of her wet bra hitting the dock. She leaned her head back on his shoulder and he cupped her breasts with his warm hands.

"Jesus, Gen," he whispered in her ear, taking her earlobe between his teeth and her nipples between his thumbs and forefingers. She gasped and he groaned, and suddenly, the freezing sting of the water didn't matter anymore.

They couldn't stay in the pond much longer. It was uncomfortably cold, and Chance knew he was likely to take things way too far if he didn't get the hell away from Gen's curvy, willing body immediately. Never, even in his wildest dreams, had his imagination come close to the reality of her. He hadn't planned to touch her like this, but when she was so frightened and haunted, his resolve had disappeared altogether. Cursing his weakness, he vowed to be stronger in the future. He gave her breasts one last caress, loving the way she arched into him, and then brushed his lips across her shoulder. "We've gotta get out now. Follow me."

As he placed her hands on the dock, a loud honk came from behind him. And then several things happened at once:

Something bit him hard on the shoulder, then the neck, then the butt.

That same something made the most god-awful noise he'd ever heard.

Gen screamed.

Bright lights came on.

A man shouted.

A woman shouted.

Chance found himself staring at the barrel of a large handgun.

Gen screamed again.

"What the fuck?" the man shouted.

"Put the gun away!" the woman ordered. "It's your brother."

"I can see that. What the hell is he doing?"

Chance wrapped Genny in his arms, careful to keep the murky water covering her up to her shoulders. "Put the gun away, jackass, and get her a towel," he said to his brother Will.

"Got it," Claire called over her shoulder as she sprinted to the house.

"Seriously, Chance. What are you two doing naked in my pond in the middle of the night?" Will shoved the gun in his bathrobe sash like some day spa vigilante.

"We're skinny-dipping, duh," Chance answered in his best smart-ass little brother voice.

"Wait. You told me we were trespassing," Gen said, teeth chattering.

Will glared at his brother. "You are."

"We're trespassing on your own brother's property?" She splashed his face like she'd done hundreds of times when they were kids. "That doesn't even count!"

"Well, neither does your skinny-dipping because you're still wearing clothes."

"I can fix that!" she reached down and tore off her panties and threw a mad pitch in the direction of the dock, missing his brother's head by inches.

"Whoa there!" Will said, finally breaking a smile and then chuckling.

Gen giggled, and Chance found himself bewildered. Then it hit him. She wasn't bitten by whatever got him. She didn't see the lights or the gun. She just heard all the commotion.

"Tell me we're at your middle brother's house and not the older one's."

"Yeah, it's Will's house."

"Oh, good."

Chance almost couldn't stand knowing she was completely naked and his brother was so close. An odd sense of possessiveness overcame him, but he fought it back. She wasn't his. She never would be, no matter how he wished it.

"So, nice way to spend your off time, little brother," Will remarked.

Claire arrived with two towels, and it was obvious she was fighting back laughter. "Head to the house, hon. I've got this." Surprisingly, Will did exactly as she asked, still chuckling.

She pitched Chance's boxer briefs to him. "Put those on and help me get her out. I can't wait to hear the story behind this. You're more like your brother than I thought, obviously."

Freshly showered and bundled in Claire's fleece pajamas, Gen sipped hot chocolate while Will teased Chance relentlessly, especially about the epic attack of the vicious guard swans.

"They're the best alarm system in the world—swans and geese, both," Will said. "Geese bite harder, though, so you got off easy."

Chance huffed. "Are you shitting me? That thing gave me a bruise that covers my entire ass cheek."

"Only because you're scrawny. Serves you right for fouling my waters with your nakedness," Will teased.

"Pure jealousy, brother. Clearly, you're compensating in front of your soon-to-be-bride."

"Well, swans usually aim for the soft bits, which would be a real problem for you, little bro!"

Someone punched someone and someone yelped playfully.

"Are they always like this?" Gen asked Claire, who smelled like roses and paraffin or adhesive of some kind.

"It's worse when all three of them are together. Are you warming up now?"

"I feel great. Sorry we barged in on you and woke you up."

"Oh, I was working. I'm restoring some old books that came in with an auction lot. I'm regluing bindings."

That explained the strange paraffin smell. She sniffed again. "Gunpowder?"

"Will was up, too, cleaning some target pistols. You guys spooked us, but didn't wake us." She shifted on her stool almost soundlessly. "Why don't you two stay here tonight, rather than go back to the city? We have a guest room. I've already offered the couch to Jacob. He called us when he saw the security lights go on."

She tilted her head to try to pick up Chance's reaction, but got nothing over the clock ticking on the mantle.

"Let me show you what I'm working on, Gen," Claire said, taking her hand.

She slid off the stool and followed her to a room away from the kitchen that smelled of glue and old paper. The door closed with a well-oiled *snick*.

"What's going on?" Claire asked.

"I'm not really sure," she answered honestly, leaning against the closed door.

"When I offered the guest room, Chance looked like he was going to barf. I'm guessing we're still working through the best friend's little sister prohibition? I mean, when we found you two tangled up naked in the pond, I thought Chance had finally worked past that, but maybe not?"

"Definitely not."

"Well, that sucks."

"Tell me about it."

"How can I help?"

Gen's breath caught. This woman seemed so open and caring. Maybe she really had an ally who could help her make sense of this last decade of loneliness. "You can fill in some blanks for me."

"Chance is pretty private. I'm not really that up on him.

Will's the one to ask. I'll make sure you get a chance to speak with him alone soon." She brushed some hair behind Gen's shoulder. "What were you two doing in the pond—besides some obvious grab-ass?"

"I've persuaded him to help me complete a ten-year-old bucket list."

"Oooh. Nice. Tell me about that. I think I have a plan working."

"So, Walter's little sister, huh?" Will slid up to sit on the kitchen counter and folded his arms over his chest. "It's about time."

Leaning against the counter, Chance lifted his hands in surrender. "It's not what it looks like."

"Like hell, it's not. Don't bullshit a bullshitter. Why would you even deny it?"

Because he had to. He dropped his arms in defeat. "I'm only helping her with some tasks. Like I told you and Michael, she has this crazy bucket list thing going."

"Are you lying because you're scared of Walter's reaction? Hell, you guys aren't even that close anymore. You've been lying to yourself for years now. How many?"

He closed his eyes, tired of the constant battle for control over himself and the situation. How easy would it be to give up and give in finally? To profess the love he'd hidden forever. But he couldn't. It wasn't fair to her. She could do so much better. He'd never be what she needed. "Ten."

"Ten years. Roughly a third of your life. You going for half? Waiting until she gives up on you and hooks up with someone else?"

The thought of someone else touching Gen made his fingers curl into fists. Will obviously didn't miss that fact and gave a pointed nod to his hands still balled at his sides. "I thought so." He slid down from the counter. "Claire has a favorite saying, 'Use your dick, don't be one.' From the looks of things in the pond, you're on the right track."

"I made a promise to Walter."

"Yeah. I know. And what did Walter promise in return? Not a damned thing." He reached out and squeezed Chance's shoulder. "You and I both know what happened ten years ago, and he doesn't have a fucking clue. Hell, I bet you haven't even told Genny. I play racquetball with him every other week. He talks about you like you're one step from the edge and his sister like she's made of blown glass. You and I know better. You're solid, and that woman's tough."

A door at the back of the house opened and women's laughter drifted into the kitchen.

Will punched his shoulder to get his attention. "Hey, little brother. Use your dick. Don't be one. You deserve happiness. So does she. Make this right, okay?"

Chapter Eleven

Gen couldn't believe she was actually heading to the Bahamas. Chance had reluctantly agreed to go to their private island early for wedding prep after Claire's relentless urging, but she knew he hadn't been happy about it. He and Will discussed paperwork for an upcoming auction from seats near the back of the tiny cabin of the Anderson Enterprises jet, while Claire translated some scrolls, and Gen wondered what the hell she was going to do with her life from here.

She was surprised Walter didn't make more of a stink about her going, but evidently, Will held some sway with him and he'd agreed. God, it pissed her off that he controlled her money and her life. She wasn't helpless, nor was she stupid. Somehow, she needed to get her family on board with that—should have done it years ago, but the timing had never seemed right. It was always easier to just keep the status quo.

She yawned, hoping no one noticed. She'd waited last night for Chance to come to bed after he agreed to stay in Will and Claire's guest room, but he never made an appearance. When he was nowhere to be found the next morning, Claire told her that he had borrowed Will's motorcycle to go home to get clothes for the trip since his big brother was so much bigger and nothing fit.

Fortunately, except for Gen's much larger chest, Claire was close to her size, so she was totally set, including a lovely silky-feeling dress for the wedding that she was told had a tropical print perfect for the island. Since all she had were the clothes she wore to skinny-dip, Claire also lent her a swimsuit, shorts, several shirts, and flip-flops.

Between the hum of the engines and the buzz of the men's voices as they discussed transactions, her eyelids became too heavy to hold open.

Chance jumped from his seat at the back of the plane when Gen screamed his name during touchdown.

Still sound asleep, she thrashed in her seat. "Oh, God, Chance! Help me!"

He knelt in front of her and wiped away her tears, then pulled her to him. "Right here, baby. Hang on to me. I've got you. You're safe."

The engines roared as they slowed their taxi on the runway. Her breaths came in huge gulps as if she were drowning. She flinched, then wrapped her arms around him so tightly he could hardly breathe, then practically climbed his body. "Chance!" she screamed again. He held her against his chest as he waited for her to come out of the nightmare. Over her shoulder, he met his brother's eyes.

He buried his face in her hair and inhaled, wishing things were different. That he could go back and change things. So many things.

A strong hand squeezed his shoulder. "Make this right," Will said as he exited the plane with Claire.

How? How the fuck was he supposed to make this right? He turned to watch his brother and his future wife disappear down the stairs to the tarmac. It was his fault Genny had fallen in the water in the first place. He could never go back and be there for her. If he could, he would. He'd lived that night a million times a year—for ten years. Always with regret.

She whimpered and clung tighter, like she was hanging on to the piling waiting to be saved. How often did she have this nightmare? he wondered. Would she have it the rest of her life?

"I'm here, Genny," he whispered, not bothering to wipe away his own tear as it made its way down his cheek. "I've always been here. I always will be."

"I knew you'd come," she said with a sigh, and then her breathing slowed and her grip loosened.

He stroked her hair for several minutes while she slept, and eventually, her eyes fluttered open, unseeing, thank God, or she'd have witnessed him completely undone. "Hey, Gen." He was surprised his voice was so solid. "We're here."

"Oh." She sat up straight and cocked her head. "I must have dozed off."

"You sure did, sleepyhead." He helped her to her feet. "I have good news, though. We're about to knock another item off your list."

She smiled, and his skin warmed like the sun had come out. "Really?"

"Absolutely. Right now, we're on a bigger island, but later, we'll travel to my family's private island by speedboat. First, though, I have strict orders from Claire to take you undergarment shopping since hers didn't fit you."

A furious blush crawled up her cheeks. "I can do that without your help."

"Yes, well. You see, I have this bucket list of my own now, and this happens to be on it."

"What? Buying me underwear?"

"No. Not getting my ass kicked by my future sister-in-law."

She laughed and let him help her down the plane's steps.

"Don't let her sweet demeanor fool you. Claire's fierce. She has to be in order to put up with Will."

"Where are they?" She turned her face into the sea wind, listening and taking in the smells, no doubt.

"They're running some errands, but said they'll join us for dinner."

Her brow furrowed. "It's still before lunchtime."

Placing his hand at the small of her back, he applied gentle pressure, and she followed his lead across the tarmac to where a car was waiting. "Sadly, you're stuck with me for the day."

"Ah. I'll just have to make do."

The driver, whom he'd never met before, opened the car door, and Chance guided Gen into the vintage Town Car. She took a breath and wrinkled her nose at the less-than-sparkly interior. It was posh by island cab standards.

"After some shopping, we'll go straight to our island. I can't believe I've never had you here. This should have happened long ago."

She shook her head. "You tried. Your whole family tried. My parents thought it was too dangerous for me."

Prickles of anger crawled up his spine and lodged at the base of his skull. His lifestyle might not be right for her, but neither was the one her family imposed upon her. She'd lived her young life like a bird in a cage. He'd always hated it. Which was why he'd insisted Walter allow her to tag along everywhere they went. He exhaled a deep breath. "Well, you're here now."

When the car took off, she reached in his direction and patted her way across the torn leather seat until her hand made contact with his thigh. His breath caught, muscles tensing at her touch, and she momentarily paused. Then her fingers glided up the outside of his hip to his chest, and finally his face. Her second hand joined the first as she took measure of his expressions, just like she'd done when they were younger.

She faced him on the seat, tilting her head in that questioning, curious way she had. "You never used to tense up when I touched you. It's like I make you uncomfortable now."

He smiled, and her fingers gently explored his dimples and the corners of his eyes, then brushed over his jaw. "Your whiskers have gotten harder. So have the angles of your face... And your muscles."

And other parts as well...

She asked, "Why is my touch different to you now?"

He reached down and ran his palm up her bare thigh, stopping at the hem of the denim shorts she had on over a swimsuit. He smiled when she jerked. "Because of that." Because for ten years, he'd thought of little else but her. Because he no longer took her for granted or expected her touch. It was always a surprise now. A gift. And a massive turn-on, rather than just a communication.

It was different because he loved her. Not as her big brother's best friend, but as a man. *Make this right,* Will had told him twice. As he looked at her beautiful, brave face he wondered if finally, that might actually be possible—that things could be right. That he could show her the adventure and freedom she craved so badly and still keep her safe.

"We're here," the driver said in his thick accent. "Do you want me to wait?"

Chance pulled Gen's hands from his face and kissed the inside of both palms, loving how her breath stuttered and her eyes widened. "No. We're good from here on. Thank you."

Something had changed since they boarded the plane. Gen didn't know what it was, but Chance acted different. Maybe his brother had said something, or maybe it was what happened in the pond. The way he'd cupped her breasts in his palms. Even now, the thought of it made her nipples harden and her lower body ache. Or maybe it was simply being far enough away from Walter that allowed him to drop the decade-old wall he'd erected between them.

Whatever it was, she liked it. He was playful and teasing at the lingerie shop, describing in great detail and with obvious relish the finer points of each garment, and he was relaxed and chatty all through lunch as well. She brought one of the palms he'd kissed earlier to her flushed face and sighed as the waiter cleared their dishes.

"Ready to go knock speedboat off the list?"

Her grin must have been answer enough because in no time, they walked hand in hand down a wooden pier, her cane folded neatly in the shoulder bag Claire had lent her before boarding the plane.

He stopped and took her bag. "Here, in the Bahamas, this kind of boat is sometimes called a rumrunner, but in most places, this is called a cigarette boat...sometimes, a go-fast boat."

"Offshore racing boat," she said.

"Not this one. It's smaller than the real racers and not equipped for that kind of speed, but yes. That's the kind of boat we're dealing with here."

"I know this already. Why do you think speedboat made my list? Walter wouldn't shut up about it after he came here with you and your brothers your senior year before I... Before you..."

When he spoke, his voice sounded strained. "That was a

long time ago. This is a different boat."

And she was a different person. "Is it faster?"

"Yes."

"Good."

After strapping on a life vest, she cautiously let him guide her across the front of the boat and into the left seat. "What do you see?"

He slid in next to her. "A beautiful, sunny day, a fast boat full of gas, and a beautiful woman."

"Seriously. What does this look like?"

"You're seated in a Baja Outlaw. It's primarily white with yellow and black accents. GPS is in front of you. Steering wheel, throttle, and controls are on the right, in front of me."

"Have you done this before?"

"Many times. We'll take it easy, though, okay?"

"Why?"

There was a pause for a moment, and she could feel his eyes on her as he spoke. "Good question. If you want to go fast, I'm up for it."

"I'm up for anything!" she said. "Everything."

"One order of everything coming right up."

The motor growled to life, and after a few minutes of cruising slowly, to get out of the harbor, she assumed, Chance picked up speed. Before long they were flying, sometimes literally, over the water. The sensation of speed with the wind whipping around her and the constant roar of the motor was unlike anything she'd experienced, and she laughed. She laughed and laughed as they cut through the water, bouncing over waves so fast, she could feel her skin pull tight. She was still laughing when he slowed and the motor grumbled then went silent.

"What happened?"

"Nothing. I just wanted to take a break for a minute."

"Are we to China yet?"

"Not yet."

"What do you see?"

"Nothing but bright blue ocean." He brushed his fingers across her knee and she startled. "And you. I see you, Gen."

She held her breath as waves lapped the side of the boat, and somewhere overhead a bird screeched.

The boat rocked slightly, forcing a nervous gasp from her lips. "What are you doing?"

"Taking off my clothes. Let's swim."

There was a *click*—probably a life vest clasp, followed by a rustling of fabric and the unmistakable *zing* of a zipper. Like the one on his shorts.

"Naked?"

"Of course."

"Here?"

"There's no one around for miles. This is skinny-dipping Anderson style."

She turned her face toward him, hoping her shock didn't show. He'd always been so free and reckless. It shouldn't surprise her he would do something like this, but it felt completely uneven from where she sat. "I wish I could see."

The air shifted in front of her as he positioned himself between her and the dash, then his hands were on her shoulders. "I don't."

"Why?"

"Oh, Gen. If you could see, you'd be like everyone else." His breath fanned across her lips, and it was all she could do to not lean into him and close that gap. "If you could see, you wouldn't be here with me right now, and I wouldn't be able to do this."

His lips were soft and gentle. Nothing at all like the hungry, needy clashing of bodies on the bench at Columbus Circle yesterday. Heart racing, she gripped the arms of the boat's bucket seat, headily aware he was naked and worried she'd accidentally grab a handful of heaven if she wasn't careful.

"Relax, Gen. No one can see us. It's just you and me. Walter will never know. I'm only going to kiss you." Her grip on the chair loosened slightly, and he kissed her again. His movements were leisurely, and their tongues danced together as if they had all the time in the world, and with the warm sunshine and the waves gently rocking the boat, it seemed to her that maybe they did.

He'd propped his hands on her seat on either side of her head, and nothing touched but their mouths. She was so attuned to him, it was easy to know where he was. From the pressure of his palms on the cushion to the heat of his skin, she could imagine his long, lean body kneeling in front of her, and it filled her with power.

Releasing her grip on the chair, she wrapped her arms around his ribs and ran her fingers over the taut skin and powerful muscles of his back. He moaned deep in the back of his throat, and it set off a crazy chain reaction of fireworks in all the right places in her body, leaving her achy and hot. Whatever he did at that martial arts gym made his chest and torso hard as a rock with no extra anything anywhere. After scraping her nails slightly over his skin, she ran her hands across his scalp and fisted his long hair in her fingers. He let loose a growl, which set off a wave of need so strong inside her, she growled right back, arching to get closer, to get more of him.

From somewhere behind them, a phone rang, and Chance pulled away. "My God, Gen," he rasped, breath harsh, nearly panting. "It's a good thing number ten is taken care of, because sex with you would probably kill me outright. Kissing you is almost too much."

She didn't know whether to be flattered or disappointed. She'd made out with guys before. Several of them once she was out of her parents' house, but never had there been a reaction like this, either from her own body or from the guy she kissed.

This was different. Like she'd always known it would be with him.

The ringing stopped, then immediately started again. "There's only one person that persistent," Chance said, standing up. The boat rocked as he stumbled to the back, cursing the entire way. "What?" he answered harshly. "Yeah, Michael. My cell was off for a reason: I didn't want to be interrupted... You knew that? And so you call the fucking satellite phone on the boat? What's on fire?" He went quiet for a moment. "Oh, you don't like my tone? Well call me back and we can start over." He slammed the phone down on something metal.

"Is something wrong?"

"Nah. Michael's just being an uptight prick and we're playing our usual games."

A rustle of fabric followed by a *zing* of a zipper told her he'd likely put on his shorts again.

The phone rang again, and he answered it in a sickeningly sweet voice. "Michael's doormat service. How may we meet your foot-wiping needs today?... Yeah, I'm hilarious..."

Gen relaxed back in her seat, enjoying this side of Chance she'd never seen before. She loved hearing him interact with his brothers.

"What am I doing? Well, actually, I'm right in the middle of an intense game of shuffleboard, why?...No, I'm not on the island. I'm about ten miles offshore....Yes, it's inconvenient. I can't even tell you how fucking inconvenient..."

She couldn't help but giggle.

"Oh, but yes, King Michael. Anything for you." He didn't slam the phone down as hard this time, but he was still a bit rough.

"We'll have to swim later," he said, buckles snapping as he put on his life vest.

"What happened?"

"Some mix-up with a delivery date, and evidently, a tent for the wedding is being dropped off early. Will and Claire are still on the big island, and someone has to be at our place to sign for it or they'll take it away and Michael's freaked they won't get it back in time for the wedding."

"That's cool. No big deal," she said, trying not to let her disappointment show.

"I'm really sorry."

"Truly. No big deal."

"How about you drive back?"

"Holy shit, Chance. I can't do that."

"Sure you can. We're in open water. I know this place like the back of my hand. You can't possibly wreck or damage anything, and I'll work the throttle. You'll just steer and I'll tell you where to go."

The chair squeaked as he sat in the driver's seat. "Scoot over here and sit in my lap."

Well, that was something she wasn't going to pass up. Even if it meant having to drive the scary, fast boat.

Reaching toward him, she met his hand, and he helped her up and over to his seat. Careful not to fall, she lowered herself onto his lap and gasped as he pulled her back against his seriously prominent erection. He bucked his hips slightly and she squeaked, then laughed.

"Mm-hmm. No big deal, huh?"

The motor rumbled to life, and she squealed as he placed her hands on the steering wheel. "Just put your hands at ten and two and keep it straight. I'm right here."

"Yeah, I noticed," she said, nudging back against him. He groaned, then shifted the motor into gear, slowly gaining speed, making the wind whip her hair in all directions.

"Now turn the wheel a bit so you can feel how it responds."

Gradually, she eased the wheel right, then left, feeling the boat tilt toward the turn. "I'm really doing it!" she said. "I'm driving."

"Yes, you are."

"Oh, Chance. I never..." Tears of joy dried before they even breached the edges of her eyes as they zipped over the water. The powerful boat rumbled under her feet and through the steering wheel into her hands; she relaxed against Chance's trim, hard body.

This was who she was. This was living.

Chapter Twelve

"What do you see?" Gen asked as Chance tied the boat off behind the party supply delivery company's boat at their private pier.

What did he see? *Red.* He'd never been this pissed at Michael before. Not even when his big brother had teased him about getting braces, or when he'd sent him to go sober Will up after a bender before he'd worked things out with Claire.

This was not at all how he'd thought the day would go. He'd planned to get Gen relaxed and show her what real skinny-dipping was like. To let her float in the warm ocean, far from anyone or anything, and feel freedom for the first time.

"Chance?"

He stepped back into the boat and guided her to her feet. "I see a small, private island owned by my family. There are a dozen brightly colored buildings with thatched roofs, white sand, and clear blue water." Leading her up onto the front deck of the boat, he held her hands while she caught her balance, then helped her to the edge of the bow and the safety of the pier. "I see a guy holding a clipboard coming toward us from a pile of poles and canvas on the beach."

And in his mind, he saw himself delivering a well-placed kick to Michael's perfectly shaven face for ruining his afternoon.

She pried his fingers from hers. "Loosen up." She took his wrist and shook it until his hand was pliant and relaxed, then laced her fingers through his. "That's better. Did my driving scare you that much? I mean, I let you take over when we got to the parking part."

Perhaps the afternoon hadn't been that wasted. She seemed to love driving the boat. Maybe more than she would have enjoyed skinny-dipping—but not nearly as much as he would have. He scanned her incredible body and bit back a groan.

"Mr. Anderson!" the man in a Hawaiian shirt called as he stepped onto the pier. "Thanks for meeting me. Seems there was some kind of mix-up on timing."

He signed the paper on the clipboard. "No problem."

"The crew will be here to set up in the morning." His eyes roved up and down Gen's body, and Chance's muscles readied like they did before a match. She tilted her head as if she could tell something was up, but she said nothing.

"Well, thanks again for meeting me. Sorry for the confusion."

As he got in his boat and pulled away from the pier, Chance realized he couldn't blame the guy, really. Gen looked great in that loaner pink bikini top that didn't cover even half of her, *thank you, Claire*, and cutoff blue jeans with her hair all windblown and tangled from the boat. It was *his* reaction that was troubling. This type of possessiveness was new. Hell, this whole situation was new. Over the past ten years, he'd denied himself access to her—held back by the fear he was bad for her. Now, he was completely alone on an island with her, and somehow that fear didn't hold the weight it used to.

It didn't hold any weight at all, in fact, as it lifted like a helium balloon and drifted away in the ocean breeze ruffling the fine hairs around her face. Maybe her stifling, cautious lifestyle was even more dangerous to her than his adventurous one.

Will's voice pierced his thoughts. *Make this right.*

"So, how about that swim Michael rudely interrupted?" he asked, leading her up the pier toward the island. "Not quite as cool as being in open water, but I can promise no attack swans."

"Sounds good."

He went hard...well, harder. Gen at his island...with him...naked in the sunshine. Life didn't get better. "We'll need some towels and suntan lotion. Follow me."

As they hit the soft sand, she stopped. "Hey, Chance?"

"Yeah?"

She cocked her head to the side. "Remember that game we used to play?"

"Marco Polo?"

"No, challenge."

"Was that an official game? I thought it was just us daring each other to do crazy things like eat dog food or freeze Walter's underwear."

"Or how about that time I challenged you to shave your legs?"

He laughed. "I didn't know to use water and soap and used my mom's razor dry. I had a rash for a week. Will still gives me shit for that."

"Hey, Chance?" She took his hand in hers. "Ready for a challenge?"

"What if I refuse?"

"Then you have to answer a question truthfully."

"What's the challenge?"

"Kiss me."

He dropped both bags in the sand and took her face in his hands. "Challenge accepted."

Chance tasted like salt and ChapStick and sunshine. Gen moaned as he fisted one hand in her hair and trailed the other down the center of her spine, then cupped her backside and pulled her tight against him. The feel of the hard ridge of his erection against her belly set her on fire. Ten years she'd been missing him. Ten long years.

He tilted her head and groaned as he deepened the kiss, taking her mouth with possessive, hungry desperation she totally understood. His hand roved up her back and down again, fingers tracing the waistline of her shorts, then sweeping up to untie her swimsuit top. Her breasts sprang free and she gasped in surprise.

"Too much?" he asked, pulling away.

"Not enough." *Never enough.*

She could feel his eyes on her, so she straightened her shoulders to give him a better view. With the tips of his fingers, he traced the underside of her breasts, then wrapped his arms around her, again covering her mouth with his.

She'd been told she had a good body. She knew her chest was larger than most because even her mother had remarked on it, but Chance had never said a thing about it one way or another. Now he didn't have to. He was showing her as he slid his hands under the suit in the front and took her breasts in his hands, never breaking the kiss.

He pulled back slightly, hands still cupping her, thumbs roving over her nipples making her knees week. "God, Gen."

He kissed the hollow behind her ear, then trailed his tongue down her neck to her shoulder while her fingers explored his back and shoulders.

"Suntan lotion," he said. "We're going to burn, and that would be bad."

"Don't care," she murmured, dizzy with lust from the slow circles of his thumbs across her nipples.

"It would mean no more touching."

She pulled away and grinned. "Suntan lotion, then." She placed her hands over his and pushed up to plump her breasts, which based on his groan, appealed. "Then more of this."

"Challenge accepted." The promise in his voice caused chills to dance along her spine.

"What do you see?" She held her breath for his answer.

"My wildest dreams."

Gen waited for Chance on the porch of the main house while he went in search of towels and suntan lotion. She'd been unhappy when he'd told her Will and Claire were not joining them until dinner. She'd hoped to ask Will some questions before she took this thing with Chance any further.

Maybe she should just ask Chance what she wanted to know—why he'd abandoned her for ten long years. What had really happened that night when he'd left her alone on the dock for so long and hadn't followed her to the hospital.

She traced her finger on the edge of the wicker table, took in a deep breath of ocean air, and shook her head. He'd probably tell her it was because he'd promised her brother he would stay away. Or maybe he'd say he was bad for her, like he had earlier. How could someone who made her feel so alive be bad for her? There was something he wasn't saying.

"Taa daa!" She flinched at his enthusiastic entrance.

"Success. Towels, sunscreen, and a cold beverage. Can't beat that." His footsteps on the wooden porch stopped, and she knew he had sensed her unease. "What's going on?"

"Why did you leave?"

The chair next to her scraped as he pulled it out from under the table. "To get sunscreen and towels..."

"For ten years."

"Oh..." A nearby scrape indicated he'd moved his chair right next to hers. "You know the answer. I was forbidden to see you."

"You still are."

"Turn around." He scooted his chair even closer.

She sat sideways and waited while he rubbed lotion between his palms, then smoothed it over her shoulders. "I've made lots of mistakes in my life. Some are unforgivable." Using his thumbs, he kneaded the knots in her shoulders and she bit back a groan, fighting to concentrate on his words and not on the crazy party going on in her body because of his touch. "But I'm asking for your forgiveness nonetheless."

His hands slid lower as he smoothed lotion across her shoulder blades.

"Even though I don't deserve it." Chills skittered up and down her spine as, still seated behind her, he ran his hands down the outside of her arms, then back up, distributing lotion and a heavy dose of sexual tension. After squeezing more in his palms, he traced his hands over her shoulders and across her clavicle, pulling her back against his bare chest. "Forgive me, Genny."

She relaxed her head back on his shoulder and sighed as he rubbed lotion over the exposed skin of her chest, then moved his hands lower to her belly, teasing the waistband of her shorts, sending every nerve in her body humming. "Let me make it up to you," he whispered, hands roaming back up her body to cup her breasts, then sliding under the suit to apply sunscreen to her sensitive skin. He pinched a nipple and her body jerked, a hiss escaping her lips as he rasped her earlobe between his teeth.

It was impossible to sit still with his hands and mouth roaming over her, setting her on fire. "Chance..." She squirmed, needing more.

Clearly he got the message, because he deftly unbuttoned her shorts, slipping the zipper open, and she bit her lip in anticipation as he toyed with the elastic top of her swimsuit bottom.

"You've had me hard all day, Gen. Are you wet?"

His frankness startled her. And thrilled her, causing a warm flush between her legs. None of the guys she'd kissed had ever been this forward. Maybe because she'd been tense. Maybe because they were focused on the fact that she was blind...

He slid his hand down the front of her suit, and she stiffened at the amazing sensation of his touch, which felt nothing like when she touched herself.

"Mmmm. You are," he murmured, shifting so that his legs were on either side of her chair, making her feel surrounded by him. Cocooned and completely safe. "Relax," he whispered, stroking his finger over her most sensitive spot, causing heat to rush through her entire body and her back to arch.

"So responsive." He sought that point again, and she almost cried out as he pressed down and made perfect, electrifying circles with his finger until she gasped for air.

"Chance."

"I'm right here." He dipped his finger into her wetness and smoothed it over her, resuming that maddening pressure and speed at her core, even as he cupped her breast with his other hand and gave her neck an openmouthed kiss.

One guy had stuck his hand down her pants before, and a

couple of others had groped her breasts, but none had come even remotely close to this. Those times had been awkward and sometimes pleasant, but not…this. This was magic. Like something out of those movies Sherry loved where everyone screamed and moaned a lot and came so easily—which, until this moment, she'd thought was total fantasy.

He increased the pressure and pace, and she found herself thrusting into his hand as he whispered encouraging words against her neck.

Nothing could be this good. This intense.

Not letting up at all between her legs, he pinched her nipple, and she groaned again. Then he bit down slightly on her neck and that was it.

In a moment that bordered on surreal, she tumbled over that edge into complete bliss that went on and on. Wave after wave of pleasure washed through her as she shouted who knew what and thrashed her head from side to side against his shoulder. It was an I've-waited-for-you-for-ten-years climax, that—had there been such a thing—would have gone in the Mother of All Orgasms Record Book.

When her body finally floated back down to earth, she relaxed completely against him and sighed. Then giggled. And giggled some more until they were both laughing. She loved the rumbly sound of his laughter as she leaned back against his chest.

"That sunscreen should come with a warning label," she said.

"*You* should come with a warning label." He brushed some hair from her sweaty face. "Like those blue pill ads on TV… 'May cause prolonged erections.'"

She snorted, and they both laughed again.

"I have a challenge for you, Gen."

"Bring it."

"I challenge you to put this sunscreen on my back without

touching anything but my back."

"That's a weird challenge."

"Not really. I want to swim, and if you touch me anywhere else, we'll be heading into that house and not coming back out for many hours."

"You say that like it's a bad thing."

"It's bad if you want to complete the next item on that list today. Hands please."

She extended her hands palm-up. He placed the sunscreen in one hand and a bottle of something in the other.

She lifted the bottle up. "What's this?"

"Spin the bottle, of course. Drink up."

Chapter Thirteen

Chance fastened his top button and swept the hair out of his eyes.

"So, why'd you put on a shirt if we're going swimming?" Gen asked as they crossed the beach together, walking so close they bumped each other like they used to when they were younger. If he kept a straight line and constant speed, she didn't need a cane or to hold on to him. The powdery white sand was obstacle-free, so she could easily navigate. He loved moments like this in which she had autonomy. He'd actually whooped out loud when he found out she'd moved out of her parents' house and into an apartment of her own two months ago. A woman like this needed to spread her wings, not be separated from the world by safety glass.

"Because we're playing spin the bottle first, and fair is fair. You have on two items of clothing, and now so do I."

"It's going to be a short game with only two."

"It seems like an unfair game anyway," he said, stopping under the shade of a cabana erected near the water. "At least for you, it seems unfair. It's visual. Players get to see each other with their clothes off."

She took a large swallow of the beer he'd given her, and the movement of the muscles in her throat mesmerized him. "You're assigning way too much value to the sense of sight in this game. I'm going to enjoy this every bit as much as you." She finished off the beer and handed him the bottle, then tilted her head. "You didn't drink one, did you?"

"No."

"Andy, my bartender friend, says you never drink at all."

"I don't."

"You used to in high school. A lot."

"I swore off alcohol a while back."

"And it doesn't bug you that I drink?"

"Not at all. It's a matter of excess. You drink socially and for pleasure. I drank to get drunk. Period. I know myself well enough to know when it's wise to step up or step back."

She reached out and touched his face, tracing his features. As she ran her fingertips over his lips, he kissed them, and she grinned. He pulled her to him in a hug and kissed the top of her head. "Time to play. Prepare to lose."

He spread a large beach towel on the sand under the thatched-roof cabana and smoothed the area in the center, placing the bottle on its side. Not ideal spinning conditions, but it would be a short game, so it would have to do. "Ready?"

"Always." She shuffled closer, feeling for the towel with her toes, then leaned down to locate the bottle and a place to sit, nearly spilling her breasts out of the swimsuit. Chance took a deep, controlled breath and bit back a groan. *A very short game.*

"So, who spins first?"

"You do."

She grinned and found the bottle. Then gave it a twirl. Because of the soft sand and towel, it only spun a half turn, straight at him. She leaned forward and ran her hands over the bottle, then sat back triumphant. "You lose. Take something off, Anderson."

"Oh, no. We're playing your game, but we're playing it my way. Winner gets to take the item off of the loser."

"Oooh. I like it." She crawled closer, then swept her hands out on the towel until she made contact with his knee. Sitting back on her heels, she tilted her head. "So how do we determine what comes off first?"

"Ordinarily, you start with the least revealing." He placed her hands on his chest. "Start with my shirt."

Fascinated, he watched her face as she unfastened his top button, then the next. As if nervous, she licked her lips, and her eyebrows drew together in concentration. "It's weird to undo a button from this side. It's very different from unbuttoning my own."

Obviously, she wasn't in the habit of undressing people, despite the fact that she was a skilled kisser and had responded so enthusiastically to his touch back on the porch.

He throbbed just thinking about holding her as she went off, calling his name in that breathless, mindless way. How had he managed to stay away this long? Why?

After freeing the last button, she swept her hands inside his shirt and across his chest, then pushed it over his shoulders and down his arms. He lifted his hands free of the sleeves, pitched the shirt aside, and then leaned back on his elbows, waiting to see what she'd do. "This is where the sighted person has an advantage."

"Wanna bet?" She crawled closer, placing her knees at his side, and reached toward him. He held his breath, fascinated as she tentatively ran her fingers up his sternum. He released his lungs on a whoosh as her other hand joined the first and she swept them out across his chest, then down his abdomen, stopping above the navel.

"Your skin is smooth."

"Did you expect warts or scales?"

She laughed. "No, but your muscles are so hard underneath the skin. It's...not what I expected."

Which made him wonder what kind of guys she'd been with. "It's the result of many hours in the dojang."

"That's your martial arts gym."

"Yes."

He closed his eyes as she set her hands in motion again, sweeping up his stomach and fanning across his pecs. His muscles contracted as she brushed his nipples.

"Oh." She grazed them again, and he sat upright. "Oh, that's cool. Yours are sensitive like mine." She leaned forward and touched the tip of her tongue to his nipple, and he groaned. "I love this game," she said.

It was about to be the shortest game in history if she licked him again. He'd have her on her back on that towel in a matter of seconds if she kept this up. "My turn."

He spun the bottle and it went one and a quarter times around to point right at her, seated by his side. She reached out and located the mouth of the bottle and frowned. "I was hoping to get to see the rest of you."

"The game isn't over yet."

She reached behind her neck to unfasten the top of her suit, but he brushed her hands away. "My job, remember?"

That lifted her mood, and when her breasts bounced free of their restraint, she sighed.

He sat back and simply stared in awe. She was perfect. Her large, high breasts rose and fell with her rapid breaths, nipples erect and just waiting for attention. Attention he planned to give them, but not just yet. "Your turn."

Her brow wrinkled in confusion.

"You're underestimating the sense of sight. Just seeing you makes me so hard it hurts."

She grinned and spun the bottle, straight at him, of

course.

"Come see for yourself."

Her breasts jiggled as she crawled toward him, and he bit back a curse. Fuck, she was hot. And fun. And smart. But as she reached for him, she hesitated, only for a moment, but long enough to raise his suspicions. And when she trembled as she fumbled with the button on his shorts, she confirmed those suspicions.

He stayed her hands, then pulled them to his chest over his heart. "Number ten is still in play, isn't it?"

She didn't say anything, but turned her head away.

If she was still a virgin, it was a game changer. He needed to slow way down and let her take it at her speed, and on her terms.

"Gen. It's me. We've always been honest with each other."

"No, we haven't. You weren't honest with me for ten years. I'm not sure you're truly being honest with me even now."

"I have never ever lied to you." He'd lied to himself. But no more.

He popped the button on his fly and unzipped his shorts and pulled them off, then took her hand and placed it on his hardened flesh. "Look. See how you affect me. How much I want you."

Tentatively at first, she explored him with her fingertips, face turned to the side. With gentle thoroughness, she ran the tips of her fingers over the head and across the slit as if she were reading braille. Then she explored the length of the shaft and his balls. All through her explorations, he fought to remain very still.

"It's larger than I expected."

He grinned. "Music to my ears."

Her brow furrowed.

"What's wrong?"

"It won't fit."

Her innocent frankness was the sexiest thing he'd ever experienced. "Sure it will. When the time is right." He put his hand over hers. "Please relax. This is not the time. Let's simply enjoy each other. No pressure."

"Chance." She took a deep breath. "I haven't ever... Ten is still in play."

Which both thrilled and terrified him in equal parts. "And it'll stay that way until you're sure you're ready. Whether it's a day, a week, or ten years from now."

"Not ten years," she said. "No way."

Gen loved the feel of Chance's body. All hard muscle beneath smooth, warm skin. So unlike her own softness. Foreign and mouthwatering.

She applied pressure to his shoulder. "Lie back. I'm not finished looking."

Wordlessly, he complied, stretching out on the towel in the soft sand. She knew this was taking an inordinate amount of self-control on his part. When she touched him before, his muscles strained to move—to thrust like he was designed to do. But he hadn't—he'd remained still for her. How like Chance. He'd always been that way with her. Quiet and patient.

Maybe that's why other guys seemed so awkward. They filled the space with chatter and action rather than giving her time to adjust.

Or maybe they just weren't Chance.

For as long as she could remember, she'd loved him. And then when her hormones hit in her early teens, she'd wanted him. But what was once a general longing was now a razor-sharp need.

She placed her hand over his sternum, feeling his strong, even heartbeats as they vibrated up her arm and wound through her chest. How in the world could Chance believe he was bad for her? Maybe it was guilt. Walter had always blamed him for the accident. He still did. Her stomach twisted at the thought of how furious her brother would be if he knew they were together like this.

She'd worry about the fallout later. Regardless of what they faced when they returned to real life, she had the here and now, and she was determined to make the most of it.

Starting at his neck, she began a thorough exploration of what she'd been missing for the past decade. From his wide shoulders, to the flat planes of his chest with those maddeningly sensitive nipples, to the ridged hardness of his abdomen, she investigated every inch of him, skipping the most exciting parts, because even though he was very still, his breathing measured like he was meditating, she knew it was a test for him. It certainly would be for her. Heck, if he'd been checking out her body like that, she'd have been squirming and wiggling and losing her mind—like back on the porch.

But not Chance. He indulged her even when she asked him to roll over so she could "see" his back.

Reading his body, she ran her sensitive fingers over him, shoulders, spine, even the hollows on the side of his narrow, muscular backside that made her heart hammer harder. Long thighs and hard, powerful calves. And ticklish feet. Chance was ticklish. How had she not known that?

"Enough," he gasped as he pulled his foot away, laughing. "Are you satisfied now?"

"Not even close."

He shifted on the towel, and she reached out to find him on his side, head propped on an arm, no doubt studying her the way she'd been studying him. Suddenly, she felt self-conscious.

"No way," he said. "Don't you dare get shy on me now."

She dropped her arms from where she'd folded them over her chest.

"I have a challenge for you," he said.

She lifted her chin.

"I dare you to take off that bathing suit bottom and come swim with me."

Something about touching him and feeling the power in his body had muted her bravado. Sure, she'd read about sex and sat through way too many movies with Sherry, but Chance's body naked, in real life, as opposed to her dreams, exceeded expectations and was...daunting. So was being completely bared in front of him.

"Now, listen here. I just lay perfectly still while you checked out every inch of my body. This is simply fair play. If you'd rather, you can tell me a truth."

She fought the urge to squirm. "What truth?"

He leaned close and placed his mouth against her ear. "Tell me what you were imagining as you ran your hands over my body just now."

Whoa. She was imagining all kinds of things. Amazing things from her books, from her movies, from her dreams... Things that went way past number ten and numbered in the hundreds. No way was she answering that question.

"Challenge accepted. Let's swim."

Chapter Fourteen

Chance wiped the water from his face and easily dodged Gen.

"Marco," she called, waiting for his response in the waist-deep water.

"Polo," he answered. She grinned and lunged in his direction but missed by several inches.

She was absolutely gorgeous in the brilliant sunlight, water sliding down her body, breasts bouncing as she pursued him. It was tempting to stand still and let her tag him so he could get his hands on her slick, curvy body.

When they were children, they'd played this game for hours.

"Marco." She was very close now, which was part of the fun. Seeing her response when he answered from right nearby, then dodged her tag.

"Pol—" But before he could even finish, she lunged, wrapping her arms around his waist.

She giggled, still clinging to him. "Gotcha!"

"You sure did."

And just like that, the mood shifted, and something different replaced the playful free-spirited feel of the game. He hardened against her soft curves, and she ran her hand up his back, nails lightly scraping his wet skin. Then she slid her skin against him experimentally, her thighs on either side of his leg.

"This is very different than when we played it as kids." Her voice was breathy.

He stood still as she dragged her nails down his back and over his ass, barely hanging on to the last thread of his control.

She reached between them under the water and took him in her hands. "It's a lot more fun to catch you now."

He moaned as she stroked him. "It's a lot more fun to be caught."

She stopped and turned her head.

He didn't hear anything, but then her hearing had always been much better than his. "What is it?"

"A boat motor."

Fuck. What crap timing. "That must be Will and Claire returning from their errands." Sure enough, a boat appeared on the horizon, zipping their way.

"Better get dressed," she said, disappointment clear on her face.

He wrapped his arms around her and pulled her to him. "Covering you up is the biggest waste ever. You are gorgeous, Gen. Inside and out."

And just when he didn't think she could be more beautiful, she smiled and proved him wrong.

"There's sand in my bathing suit," Gen grumbled on their way to meet Will and Claire at the pier.

"I warned you to put it on in the water."

He had, but she'd thought it would be faster to do it on the towel where they'd played spin the bottle.

Not slowing his pace through the sand, he squeezed her

hand. "I'll lick it off of you later."

Holy shit. She stopped short, and he laughed.

"I was only kidding, Gen. Sort of."

She wasn't used to sexual banter like this, or this kind of lightheartedness. Her family was so serious. It was like she couldn't find her balance. And though she loved it and found herself swept into his spell so easily, it unnerved her that his touch was so practiced. He knew exactly what to do to bring her to orgasm earlier. Exactly where to touch for the maximum impact.

Which begged the question: What had he been doing these last ten years while she mourned his loss? Why, if he found her desirable, had he disappeared from her life so completely?

She felt for his face and traced his dimples. Even his smile turned her on. But what if she'd been right all these years and he had simply moved on to better things? Perhaps the random encounter in the bar was just that—random—and she was no different to him than an item on her bucket list: a task to complete.

This wonderful dreamlike state she was experiencing might just be that: nothing more than a passing dream.

And that just might kill her.

"Is something wrong?" he asked.

"No, no… I'm fine." But she was certainly going to be warier from this point forward and not get swept away in his spell. She couldn't spend her next ten years like the last, mourning something that might have been. At least now she might get a chance to speak to Will, since Chance was clearly not going to give her any new information.

"What do you see?" she asked as they walked along the beach in the direction of the pier.

"Well, Claire's already out of the boat, and now Will's climbing out and…whoops. He just dropped the towel wrapped around his waist."

Claire's laughter drifted to them over the waves gently lapping the shore.

"Shit, Will! Cover that thing up!" Chance shouted.

"We stopped for a swim," Will answered, and Claire giggled again.

"Well, keep that towel tucked in tight. I have no desire to see your little toy squirt gun again."

"This, my little brother, is no squirt gun. It's a Super Soaker!"

Gen's cheeks heated. Her brother never joked like that.

"I thought you guys weren't coming back until dinner," Chance said.

Will chuckled. "Well, you were here all alone with a pretty woman, so I figured you might need a little brotherly advice or a tutorial."

"And I figure you might need a little brotherly roundhouse kick to the nuts."

A gentle touch guided her up the beach toward the sand. "Ignore them," Claire said. "They're cavemen."

Snorts and grunts and the sounds of wrestling came from behind them, mixed with laughter.

"What do you see?"

Claire stopped for a moment. "Two grown-up kids rolling in the sand." She put her elbow out for Gen, and they resumed their walk up the beach toward the house. "I've never seen Chance this happy. He's better every day. Will said it was pretty grim for a few years."

"What was grim?"

"Chance. His life. His future."

Gen stopped abruptly, dropping Claire's elbow.

"You don't know."

She shook her head.

"It's really not my place to say anything. I didn't know him at all until a year or so ago."

God. What had happened? She didn't know anything about what he'd been up to, other than what she'd read or heard about from friends.

"Nobody tells me anything, and I wander around in the dark, literally, hoping someone will drop a scrap of information. My parents, my brother, now you."

"You should ask Chance."

"I did. He says he stayed away because of a promise to my brother."

"That's true, and all three brothers take promises very seriously because their dad didn't, but there's more. You need to talk to Will. I'll make sure you get a chance to talk to him alone."

She grabbed Claire's arm and turned her to face her, desperate. "Please. I don't know what to do. He touches me and I melt in his hands. He talks and I believe every word. But I know… I know…" Tears stung her eyes. Freaking eyes that kept the world from her. "He'll leave, and Claire, I can't take it if he does. I can't do it again." She put her hand to her chest. "I can't hurt like that."

Claire pulled her into an embrace. "Listen to me, Gen. I don't know a lot, but I know this. He won't leave. He's still broken, and he's rebellious, even now, but if you give him a chance, he will never leave you again. That, I know. The Anderson brothers are pains in the ass, but they're fiercely loyal—to one another and to people they love."

She gave a wet sniffle against Claire's shoulder, hoping she didn't ruin her shirt.

Another round of laughter came from the brothers, followed by some loud grunts as they tussled in the sand near the pier.

Continuing toward the house, Claire wrapped an arm around her and leaned close. "Did I mention they were pains in the ass? Yep. Big, strong, silly, lovable pains in the ass."

Chapter Fifteen

Gen's sides hurt from laughing. All through dinner, Will and Chance entertained them with stories about their antics growing up. Now they'd moved on to tales of adult shenanigans.

"And then..." Will said, pausing to catch his breath. "Then we go to Michael's apartment, prepared to do an intervention."

"...because Will was convinced he was some kind of sex addict," Chance added.

"The tabloids said that, I didn't."

"Anyway—"

"Anyway, we go in there, and Mighty Mikey's in his underwear—" Will broke out laughing again, slapping his hands on the table.

Chance took up his sentence, laughing between words. "...holding this froufrou dog in his lap—"

"...crying his eyes out over Mia, because she'd figured out he was a controlling jackass and told him to take a hike." Will snickered. "It was pathetic."

"Not as pathetic as the butt-ugly matching homemade

sweaters he and the dog had on when he proposed!"

"Those *were* pretty terrible," Claire agreed with a chuckle.

"I love it when Michael looks foolish," Chance said. "I wish he did it more often."

"It took guts to do what he did to win her back." Claire's voice was quieter than usual. "Sometimes that's what it takes. Putting it all out there and hoping love wins. Am I right?"

There was an awkward silence at the table, and Gen held her breath to pick up any indication of what was really going on. Will drummed his fingers, Claire's glass clinked on the table as she set it down, and Chance's foot tapped on the floor in a nervous staccato.

The tapping stopped, and Chance stood. "Well, I'd really like to do a few exercises on the beach now that the sun is down. I haven't worked out in a couple of days. Do you mind, Gen?"

"No, of course not. Go ahead."

Claire's chair scraped and dishes clattered as Chance's footsteps faded. "I've got the kitchen, Will. Why don't the two of you go out and enjoy the evening on the porch?"

There was another awkward silence in which she was certain Claire gave her fiancé a "we talked about this" look.

Will cleared his throat and tapped Gen's hand, then wrapped it over his elbow. "Claire tells me you want to talk."

She stood and allowed him to lead her out on the porch. She didn't smell Chance anywhere and heard nothing aside from the wind and waves.

"He just dropped your bags off at the small cottage, and now he's down near the water doing a warm-up. Mainly positions and punches. He'll move to kicks next." He placed her hand on the back of the chair she'd sat in earlier when Chance had applied sunscreen and his special touch. After feeling for the seat, she lowered herself in the chair, blocking heated thoughts of the two of them from her mind. She needed info before she allowed her thoughts to stray in that direction.

Metal scraped wood as Will moved a piece of furniture and sat next to her with a movement of air and a creak of wicker. "I've never seen anyone with balance as good as Chance's. Or speed. He's fucking fast. He can strike and be back in position before you even see it."

She leaned back in the chair and folded her feet under her, letting Will lead the conversation.

His voice was slightly deeper than Chance's, but had the same hint of saxophone. "When he was little, Chance would walk on the railing of our yacht like it was a circus tightrope. It scared the living shit out of my mom. And he drew. She loved that. Always said he'd be an artist. And I guess he is. Watching him fight is like watching ballet—only with more contact and sometimes blood."

She tensed, spine going rigid at the thought of Chance being hurt.

Will patted her arm. "He stopped competing a while back, so relax. He spars for fun now."

Consciously loosening her muscles, she turned her face toward Will and gave what she hoped was a believable smile, hoping he'd go on without prompting.

"Chance was forever getting into trouble, even as a little kid, because he'd get caught up in a bad situation and not fight to get out of it. Other kids weaseled out of trouble by cooking up all kinds of reasons for what they did, but not Chance. He'd stand up, take the punishment, and never make excuses."

A sharp yell came from the beach. Guttural and primal and male. Followed by another and another.

"He's doing punches. Next, kicks."

Fascinated, she turned an ear toward the sound and

spoke aloud the words she'd repeated silently her entire life. "I wish I could see him."

What would she not give, truly, to look on him with seeing eyes and take him in as the rest of the world was lucky enough to do? Her nails bit into her palms and suppressed tears stung her eyelids. She'd give anything. *Everything.*

With a deep breath, she loosened her fists, blinked hard, and squared her shoulders. *Screw this pity party.*

She'd seen Chance in a way no one else ever would. She'd seen him smile through her fingertips, his dimples sinking into his warm skin beneath her touch.

Will's chair creaked. "He's beautiful to watch. Amazing. In ten years, he's reached the top of the art. Even with my hand-to-hand combat training and my greater pounds and inches, I wouldn't stand a chance against him if I weren't his brother."

"If you weren't his brother...?"

"I could do anything to him and he would never lift a finger to me, though he could easily kill a man. That's how he rolls. There's no one in the world more loyal than Chance."

She traced the braided pattern of the wicker on the side of her chair with her forefinger. She'd never thought of Chance in this light. Loving brother, skilled fighter...

Out in the distance, the sharp shouts continued. "Is he angry?"

"No, focused. The yell focuses the energy."

"Do you watch him a lot?"

"I used to." There was a rustling as Will shifted position. "Often, he works out blindfolded. Like now."

The hairs on the back of her neck prickled. "He's blindfolded right now?"

"Yeah. I've even seen him fight blindfolded."

Why would anyone fight blind? Choose to be limited when they didn't have to be?

"At first, I thought he was doing it as penance for what happened to you at the harbor. I really did. But it's not."

More shouts from the beach.

"What is it?"

"It's his link to you, Gen. He wants a connection, and that's how he feels you."

No. He had to be wrong. She twisted her hands in the skirt of her sundress. "I don't understand."

"Neither do I, but that's the reason. I'm certain of it— even if he doesn't know it himself."

For a while, they sat in silence, listening to the fierce shouts from the beach. He was blindfolded. Deprived of the sight of the beautiful world right in front of him, just like her. *For* her.

A lump formed in her throat, but she fought against it to voice the question she'd asked thousands of times since that night all those years ago. "Why didn't he come to the hospital that night? Why did he go away for so long?"

Wicker creaked as Will shifted in his chair again. "The reason he couldn't come to the hospital is not my story to tell. It's his. As for going away, he didn't."

"Ten years."

Will's large, comforting hand wrapped over hers on the arm of the chair. "He was always there. He attended a university in the city to stay close. He had me check on you several times. He even attended your high school graduation."

She pulled her hand away. "No."

"He never broke his promise to Walter. He never approached you again, but he didn't leave. He was there, training blindfolded, trying to connect. Keeping you in his life.."

Chance's desolate voice from ten years ago tumbled through her brain. *I'm sorry, Genny.*

She covered her mouth with her hands.

"I'll tell you this, though," Will continued. "He went through a really rough patch. I don't know what he's told you..."

Her voice was barely above a whisper as she struggled to make sense of this new reality. She'd thought he'd left her behind, when he'd been there the whole time. "Nothing."

"After the business at the harbor, he spun off into all kinds of craziness. If he wasn't partying, he was attempting insane climbs or jumps—almost like he was looking to get hurt. We were really worried about him. And then one Christmas, he stopped." He snapped his finger. "Just like that. Nobody knows why. He stopped partying, toned down the dangerous sports, finished his undergrad, and went to law school. He still goes for the adrenaline, but not in a way he'll get himself killed. He comes to work every day. Works out every night. And for the past two months, he's gone to a bar in Midtown on Tuesday night to catch a glimpse of you."

He'd been there every Tuesday for two months while she'd secretly cursed him and longed for him simultaneously. He had been within reach and she hadn't even known it. "Did he tell you that?"

There was a pause, and a scrubbing sound, like someone rubbing short hair or maybe an unshaven face. Clearly, the man was uncomfortable with her question. "No, my investigator told me about the bar visits. Chance would be royally pissed I'd had him followed, so don't tell him, okay? And you know what else?"

She shook her head.

"Every day for these past two months, he's smiled more and been happier than he has in ten years."

Her thoughts spun as she tried to put the puzzle pieces in place. He'd never left. None of it fit with what she'd believed all these years.

He slapped his palms on the arms of his chair. "Well,

I'd better go in and help Claire with those dishes. Chance is cooling down now."

"Thanks. You really cleared some things up. He's lucky to have you as a brother."

"I'm lucky to have him as well." His chair scraped the floor as he stood. "He was hugely instrumental in my relationship with Claire working out. He's a good man, Gen. I want him to be happy again. I want him to make this right, you know?" Metal rasped wood as he moved the chair.

"How far is he from here?"

"If you walk straight out, you'll hit the beach. When you get to the waterline, turn left and follow it."

She stood, grinning. "You're pretty cool, Will. Most people would insist on leading me to him."

"Nobody needs to lead you two to each other. You'd find each other from opposite sides of the planet."

Chapter Sixteen

Chance heard her footsteps long before she arrived. He knew it was Gen because she walked toe-heel instead of heel-toe when she didn't have her cane, testing the ground as she walked.

The workout had cleared his head and put him more in tune with his surroundings, and himself for that matter. He timed his breathing with her footfalls. *Breathe in, step, step. Breathe out, step, step.*

Without a greeting, she dropped to the soft sand beside him, not touching, but linked by the invisible current she always emitted.

Still staring at the placid water, he broke the silence. "Did my brother fill you in on the bad years?"

She straightened the hem of her loaner sundress over her calves. "No. But he told me there were some."

"Yeah, there were."

With her finger, she traced a small circle in the sand near her knee. "Want to talk about it?"

"Not particularly." He unfolded his legs and stretched

them out in front of him toward the moon's reflection on the water. "Do you want me to?"

"Yes," she said without hesitation.

He inhaled the fresh sea air and closed his eyes. He had known this day would come eventually, but it still put him off-balance. Time to come clean. "I fell into a trap," he said after a moment. "It's a common one. People already thought something bad about me, so I made it happen."

"After the harbor."

"Because of it."

Her finger stilled mid-circle, and he looked over at her face for the first time since she joined him. Her expression was unreadable, and her skin looked translucent in the reflected moonlight. Like a dream.

Ask me, he willed her. He'd never wanted to excuse his mistakes, but he needed her to understand them. To know he hadn't willfully abandoned her that night as she believed. Not that he needed absolution. *She* did. She needed to know she mattered.

A single tear shimmered down her cheek. It was question enough.

"I didn't want to leave you on the dock. I should never have done it. It's unforgivable and I have no excuses whatsoever. Nothing that happened that night justifies that mistake."

Her only response was a slight lift of her chin.

"After we got to the end of the dock that New Year's, Phoebe called. She was crying and out of control because she couldn't reach Walter. She'd been detained by some security guards because she'd bought some weed off a guy near the cotton candy stand. She asked me to come, so I did. I don't know what she thought I could do for her, but I figured they'd let her go. I'd calm her down and help her find Walter, and it would be no big deal. Well, it turned out it *was* a big deal because they weren't security guards, they were real cops, and when I showed up, they detained me, too. Nothing would have come of it. I was totally clean. I hadn't even been drinking. But I did have a cigarette and long hair, and Phoebe acted all weird when I showed up."

Gen shifted and tucked her legs under her skirt, but still faced the water.

He folded his arms to keep from touching her, needing her warmth to soothe him. "I told the officer that I had something I had to do. That it was important, and then I'd come right back. He thought that was hilarious and told me to sit my ass down and shut up."

He closed his eyes and saw the whole thing as if it were happening in real time. "The fireworks started, and I got worried, so I told the guy again that I had to go. 'Tough shit' was his answer. I explained that I'd left a blind girl on the end of the dock and I was worried about her, and he laughed. To that point, I'd totally kept my cool, really, Gen, I had."

She placed her hand on his thigh, palm up. He slipped his hand in hers, and she squeezed. Warmth radiated up his arm to his chest.

"He said I was lying and told me to shut up. At that point, I lost my cool. I stood. I told him again, I had to go to you…actually, I shouted it, and I guess he thought I might be serious. He and another police officer decided to escort me to the dock, but said if there wasn't a girl, I was going to jail— that stoners like me would tell any lie to get out of trouble."

As if it were happening all over again, his chest tightened and his heart stuttered painfully. She placed her other hand over their clasped ones as if she knew how much he craved her touch right then.

"Before we even got close, a huge firework went off and lit everything up. You weren't there. The end of the dock was empty." He sucked in a shuddering breath and held it. "And then you screamed my name."

Her hold on his hand tightened.

"I broke away from the cops and sprinted down the dock. The bigger one caught me and I totally lost my shit. I don't remember much from there, other than punching the cop and him throwing me down, then waking up in a jail cell and calling Michael to bail me out."

She placed her hands on his face to read him, and he made no effort to hide his feelings. Regret, remorse, pain. Her gentle fingers were like a balm.

"I came to you as soon as I got out. By the time I arrived at the hospital, Walter and your parents already knew I'd been in jail for assaulting a police officer, thanks to Phoebe. The cops had let her go with no charges at all." He shook his head. "Everyone thought I'd been busted for buying dope— that you'd almost drowned because I'd left you in order to go score some drugs. I'd never been high in my life at that point. Drunk, yes, but I'd avoided everything else."

"Why didn't you tell them the truth? Why didn't you tell *me* the truth?" she asked, tracing his lips with her thumbs.

"What difference would it have made? It changed nothing. I left you on the dock. Alone. That one thoughtless act trumps everything else. I had no excuse for what I did, so I gave none."

She ran her hands over his face, but it felt more like a caress than her attempt to read his expression, and to his surprise, a slight smile tugged at the corners of her lips.

She linked her fingers behind his neck. "While we're confessing..." He ran his hands over her forearms, loving the way she leaned closer when he touched her. "I might have lured you to the dock for nefarious purposes."

"Tell me."

She arched an eyebrow and unclasped her fingers, running them through the hair at the nape of his neck. "I wanted you alone at midnight, hoping you'd kiss me."

"I was pretty sure that was your MO."

"Would you have?"

"No."

Her fingers stilled. "No?"

"I was your guardian then. Your protector."

She pulled her hands back, brow furrowed. "A protector like Walter."

"No. Never. I wanted you to experience as many things as possible. I fought all the time for you to be able to do stuff with us. I promised Walter I'd keep you safe, which is why almost killing you was such a blow."

She brushed the hair from his forehead. "You didn't almost kill me. I fell off the dock on my own. I told you I'd stay put, but I didn't."

"It doesn't undo my mistake, Gen."

"No, it doesn't, but it mitigates it. I consider us even."

He took a breath to refute her, but she stopped him with a finger over his lips.

"So, you really wouldn't have kissed me?"

"I loved you so much it hurt, but no. As attractive as you were, you were fifteen, and you were my best friend's little sister. There are lines that don't get crossed."

She drew her fingers through sand between them. "You crossed it recently."

"Yes, I did. Things changed."

"What things?"

Imagining her fingers tracing across his body, rather than in the sand, his heart kicked into high gear. "You. Me."

He took her hand and pulled it into his lap, caging it between his palms, as he worked to regain focus. He needed to finish and clear the air between them. "After the New Year's incident, things were different. The court agreed to dismiss my case if I got counseling. The shrink thought martial arts would be a good outlet for me, and she was right. While that was good, everything else was bad. Walter pushed me away, and thanks to the high school rumor mill, my classmates and their gossiping parents thought I had been busted in a drug raid and attacked a cop. Even my own parents partially bought into it."

"That's ridiculous." She made to pull her hands free, but he held them firm.

"Not by the time I was done. They already thought I was a partying loser, why fight it? I became one. I tried everything. Did everything. Blew off school, got high. And pursued women. Hell, I put Michael to shame. My bad-boy reputation opened lots of doors and bedroom windows, but it shut the ones that really mattered."

"Your brothers'."

"And yours."

Seated on the soft sand, Gen couldn't breathe, couldn't move, as Chance held her hands and heart captive.

"I never stopped thinking of you during that time. I convinced myself that you were better off without me. I bought into the notion that I was a loser and an addict. I was halfway right." He loosened his grip on her hands, but she left them between his warm palms.

"You're not a loser."

"No, but I'm an addict."

She lifted her hands to his face, finding his features relaxed.

He turned toward her, as if wanting more contact, so she obliged, placing her palms on either side of his face and not just her fingertips. "From the time I was little," he continued, "I'd binge—on adrenaline, usually, but sometimes on foods or activities. And when I went off the deep end that last semester of my senior year, I stepped off the ledge to the point of being self-destructive."

"But you aren't like that anymore. You don't drink. You have a killer job."

Under her thumbs, the corners of his mouth lifted into a gentle smile. "I still love the rush of adrenaline, though. But you're right, seven years ago I cleaned up my act. And for that, I thank you and your crazy-hot Christmas party dress your senior year of high school."

He turned his head toward the ocean and she dropped her hands, confused. *What dress?*

"Once I'd stepped away from you, I gained a better perspective of exactly who you were to me. Instead of just being my closest friend, you became my inspiration. I wanted to be like you. Be with you. Be worthy of your friendship again. Worthy enough for you to forgive me."

Again, her insides churned at the realization they'd hurt similarly.

"Suddenly, being the party guy held no appeal. After some painful false starts, I got clean, finished college, and applied to law school. The rest is history."

The sea breeze was blocked momentarily, and she sensed him stand. His soft footfalls confirmed he had moved a few steps.

She stood as well, facing the direction of the sound of hands slapping over fabric, as she imagined him brushing sand off of himself. "I don't remember a Christmas party dress my senior year."

He rested his hand on her waist. "It was red, knee-length, with a silver sequined border on the top and sequined straps. I'd never seen anything like you in that dress before."

She threw her head back and laughed. "Oh my God, Chance. That was my school choir uniform for the holiday concert. I hated that thing."

"It was hot."

"It made my boobs look huge. Everyone said so."

"I stand by my previous statement. *Hot.*"

She gave his shoulder a playful punch. "You goofball! You turned your life around because of a choir uniform!"

"I turned my life around because of *you.*"

Chapter Seventeen

Gen touched Chance's chest, and her breath hitched with surprise at his bare skin. Did he work out blindfolded *and* naked? Surely not within sight of his family. "What are you wearing?"

"I'm wearing *hai,* the loose pants I train in."

"What else?"

"Nothing else. I'm barefoot."

But he was wearing something else, and she knew it. She ran her hands up his chest and looped her finger through the stretchy fabric of the blindfold on his neck and pulled him toward her until their lips almost touched. "What else?"

His breath tickled her lips as he spoke. "Kiss me, Gen. Kiss me and tell me I'm forgiven."

Rising on her tiptoes, she met his lips and he sighed, as if with relief, then wrapped his arms around her.

She pulled back and traced his lips with her forefinger. "There's nothing to forgive—except maybe you centering a catharsis on a school choir dress. That's pretty unforgivable."

He captured her wrist, and she almost melted into the

sand when he licked the tips of her fingers. She knew he was aware how this would affect her. Many times growing up, they'd discussed how her fingers were her eyes. He then drew them into his mouth and she was unable to stand still, shifting foot to foot while his tongue slid over her sensitive skin. Too soon, he placed her hand back on his chest. "It wasn't the dress. It was the woman inside it."

"And my boobs. Come on, admit it."

Reaching between them, he ran his hands up her ribs and stopped just short of her breasts, leaving her one breath away from crazy as his thumbs traced tiny circles. "Yeah, those, too."

She groaned with relief and he smoothed his hands up her breasts, and then groaned from need when he continued those same maddeningly slow circles with his thumbs over her nipples. "Definitely those," he murmured against her neck.

He rotated her a quarter turn, and the sea breeze blew straight across her face. Her heart hammered in her ears as he untied the top of the halter sundress. Cinched with a belt at the waist, the top fell, freeing her breasts to the wind and his warm, skilled hands. There was nothing in the world like Chance's hands. He caressed her with long, strong fingers, his hands calloused, probably from martial arts. She held on to his shoulders for support, head falling back with a sigh of pleasure while his hands glided over her skin.

A sound from behind her yanked her from her haze. "Chance..."

Pulling her against his chest, he kissed the top of her head. "Just Claire closing the door. Your back is to the house and it's dark. No one can see you but me."

And just like that, she relaxed. She trusted him with everything. Her safety, her body, and her heart. No more holding back her feelings or clinging to perceived wrongs from the past. She was his, completely, and her body was in total agreement as her heart pounded and heat pooled low in her belly.

"Walk with me," he said.

"Where?"

"Farther from the house. There's a little cove a few yards away."

She reached back to tie her halter.

"No. Please don't cover yourself."

She turned her ear toward the house.

"They can only make out silhouettes, not much else. And they closed the door. There's no way they're going to come out here. They've been matchmaking since they found us in their pond. Interrupting us would be counterproductive."

"So walking down the beach half naked with you is a condoned activity?"

"Absolutely."

"I love this place." And she loved *him*. She always had, but now that she knew what had happened all those years ago, there was nothing to hold her back. Well, other than opposition from Walter, but from where she stood, that seemed too remote to worry about right then. Nothing else mattered but this amazing man.

He took her hand, and she allowed him to lead her along the waterline, loving the feel of the ocean wind and his gaze on her body.

"What do you see?" she asked when he came to a stop.

"A small, curved area of beach, protected by palm trees and a hill of white sand. It looks blue in the moonlight. And the best part? It can't be seen from the main house."

She smiled. "Are there stars?"

"To be honest with you, I hadn't noticed the sky. There's too much to look at right next to me." He ran his fingers down her jaw. "But, yes. There are lots and lots of stars."

She placed her hand on his warm chest. "Excellent. We can knock another item off the list." His muscles tensed under her hands, and she smoothed her fingers across them, fascinated. "Yeah, 'sleep under the stars' is still left."

She held her breath as he fiddled with the buckle on the belt of her sundress.

"I am not particularly sleepy right now," he said in a low, sexy voice. The belt released, and the dress slipped over her hips and fell into the sand around her ankles. The wind caressed her body, sending shivers up her spine as she waited for what he'd do next.

He started by placing his hands on her shoulders. "Not sleepy at all, in fact." He ran his palms down the outside of her arms, and when he got to her fingers, he linked his through hers. He guided her toward him, and she stepped out of the dress. "Are *you* sleepy, Gen?"

"No."

He pulled her close, and she bit back a groan as his hardness pressed against her. He placed his cheek against hers and whispered, "What do *you* see, Gen? What do you see happening from here? Tell me what you want and it's yours."

That was like telling a little child in a candy store she could have anything she wanted—as much as she wanted. Gen wanted it all. Only, nothing in her at that moment felt like a child...far from it. "Touch me."

"Where?" His mouth against her ear made her knees weak. He guided her backward until her spine contacted something solid. She explored it with her fingers. A palm tree.

"Where do you want me to touch you?" he asked, kissing a trail down her neck.

"Anywhere. Everywhere."

He slid his hands down her sides and cupped her backside. The urge to grind against him, to climb his body and wrap around him, overwhelmed her. Before she acted on that impulse, he dropped to his knees in front of her, hands still wrapped around her, and pressed a kiss to her belly. He skimmed his hands down the back of her thighs and back up again, and her knees went weak. She grabbed his shoulders for support.

Her entire body hummed with anticipation as he slid her panties down her thighs, past her calves to her feet, and then helped her step out of them, muttering words of encouragement and praise for her body that blended together in a potent lust-inducing concoction.

He stood, lifted her hands from his shoulders, and placed them above her head. "Hold on to the tree with both hands for support. Don't let go, okay?"

She nodded, gripping the narrow, rough tree trunk above her head. She liked this. Liked being so exposed to him, yet stable enough to support herself.

His lips grazed hers, and then he kissed her for real, his hands covering hers on the trunk above her head. Nothing touched except their hands and mouths, which made her body ache with longing. His skin was close enough to radiate heat to hers, and she needed to feel it. And then, just barely, his chest rubbed against her nipples, shooting spikes of desire straight between her legs. Her knees gave way, and she clutched the tree tighter to remain upright.

"Mmmm," he said as he moved one hand from hers and spread it over a breast. He traced her nipple, and she moaned.

He kissed her once more, then again lowered himself in front of her. It was easy to tell where he was, not only from the heat, or lack thereof, over her body, but because his breath fanned across her breasts and ribs.

She took a raspy gulp of air, her heart racing in anticipation. This was Chance. *Her* Chance. So familiar, yet shockingly foreign and new.

When he placed his mouth on her breast, she was sure she'd faint. Instead, she clung tight to the trunk at her back and bit her lip as his warm tongue explored her flesh, stroking and teasing.

"Chance…"

"Tell me." He caressed both breasts with his hands, kissing first one, then the other, until she was sure she'd scream.

He dipped his tongue into her belly button and she giggled, then kissed his way to her hip bone and nipped her gently. This time, she didn't giggle; she gasped as with one hand, he held her waist, and with the other, he explored the inside of her thigh, making a slow, deliberate path higher.

"I need…" And as if he'd read her mind, his hand reached the apex of her legs, fingers smoothing through her wetness, and she moaned. "*That*. I need that."

"I know, baby."

Of course he did. He knew her like no one else.

With no hesitance or prelude, he slid a finger inside and she groaned, and he slid it out, and then in again, and again. She gripped the tree for dear life when a second finger joined his first, hitting a perfect rhythm to drive her wild. And just when she thought it couldn't feel better, with the wind blowing across her nipples, still wet from his kisses, and the perfect, insistent rhythm of his fingers plunging in and out, he touched his tongue to that most sensitive spot right at the front, and she cried out.

He slipped his fingers free and she groaned.

"Shhhh," he soothed, and still kneeling, placed his hand behind one of her knees. He swung her leg over his shoulder, opening her up to him. "Keep hanging on to the tree. You can use your leg as leverage, too. You good?"

Better than good. She nodded, sure no intelligible sound would come out if she tried to talk.

This time, he placed his entire mouth over her while his tongue moved in quick flicks until her leg trembled and her nails bit into the tree.

He pulled back and her spine arched, seeking him. "So good," he said. "You taste like heaven."

This *was* heaven. She felt both weak and powerful at the same time while he kissed the thigh of the leg thrown over his shoulder. Again, his fingers entered her, and she dug her heel into his back, urging him on.

"Yes, ma'am." He chuckled. "Will do."

And he did, fingers stroking her from inside as his tongue did amazing things that caused lightning strikes of excitement to zap all through her. Her body tightened, and her breaths came in harsh gasps as she got closer.

"Mm-hmm," he encouraged, increasing his tempo.

She turned her head from side to side, loving the feel of the rough tree trunk at her back and his slick tongue on her body. But more than that, she loved *him*, and with that thought, she tumbled over the edge.

There were sounds Chance would remember forever. The way Genny called his name when she came was one of them. She'd done it twice now, and he planned to make that number much, much higher before the night was over. His beautiful Gen, glistening with sweat in the moonlight, clinging to the tree for balance. Which was a good thing. Sand was a great mood killer, which made the beach a challenge.

She relaxed, and he removed her leg from over his shoulder, then rose to his feet. She released the tree and looped her arms around his neck. With a satisfied sigh, she leaned her head on his shoulder, and he melted inside. Nothing and no one could be this perfect. He gave himself a mental pat on the back for having the self-control to stay away from her as long as he had.

"Let's swim." He shoved his pants down over his hips and stepped out of them.

She laughed. "Not sure I can walk yet."

"No problem."

When he scooped her up and cradled her in his arms to carry her to the water, she gave a feminine squeal that made his heart too big for his chest. She looped her arms around his neck and squealed again when his erection brushed her ass. "Is that your..." Her sentence died into giggles.

"My what?"

Giggles turned to a full-blown laugh by the time they were waist-deep in the warm, rolling ocean. He bent his knees so that the water lapped their shoulders. He loved her laugh. Because she'd never had sight, she didn't grow up emulating how other people looked and reacted. She laughed with her whole body, and there was nothing more beautiful.

He released her, and she stood on the bottom. He ducked under and washed his hair back from his face. When he resurfaced, she reached for him, making contact with his biceps. He stilled to give her access to his face so she could read him, but her hand ventured down, rather than up.

Her smile widened as she explored the lines of his torso, tracing left and right across the ridges in his abdomen, honed by hundreds of hours in the dojang. When her fingers came across the thin trail of hair leading lower, she stilled and tilted her head.

Swallowing hard, he controlled his breathing so as not to interrupt and allow her complete control to take things at her own rate.

Chance was hard as a rock. Without a doubt, this was the most erotic moment he'd ever experienced. She was reading him with her fingertips, as she would braille. Water lapped over their shoulders, while under the water she traced the trail of hair with one finger until she stopped at the base of his shaft. She then drew the finger up to the head and back down the underside, tracing a line around his balls. An involuntary hiss escaped through his teeth, followed by a groan as she wrapped her hand around him.

"What feels good?" she asked.

"Everything."

"Show me."

He wrapped his hand over hers and set her into a rhythm that would do the trick. When she had the hang of it, he removed his hand.

"Like this?"

"Exactly."

"Sherry narrates when we watch adult movies. She describes what's going on, but this is way better."

No shit. He gritted his teeth as her hand slid up and down beneath the water and his balls drew tighter.

"So, what would happen if I...?" She flicked his nipple with her free hand and he thrust instinctually. "Oh, that's really cool." So she did it again, eliciting the same reaction as he bucked into her hand.

Not letting up with her pumping, she kissed him like she was starving. When she made a hungry growling sound in her throat, he could no longer resist touching her and slid his hands over her breasts, then rolled her nipples between his fingers and thumbs until she was gasping for air, too.

"I've dreamed of you my whole life, Chance, but never imagined it would be like this."

His balls drew up tighter still. He was so close. "Like"— he inhaled—"what?"

If she answered, he didn't hear her. His ears rang and his body thrust into her hand as he came in wave after wave until he was disoriented and light-headed. Placing his hand over hers, he took a shuddering breath. Holy shit, what she did to him. His statement from before wasn't an exaggeration. Sex with this woman might very well kill him outright.

"Like that," she said, wrapping her arms around his body in the warm water. "Like that first big drop on the roller coaster, only better."

"Much better." He kissed her, running his hands over her body under the water. And as he looked at her beautiful face in the moonlight, he realized that no matter what happened to him from this point forward, he'd be okay. He'd always have this memory to draw on. And hopefully many more just like it. A lifetime of memories with her.

Chapter Eighteen

Chance pulled Gen closer on the makeshift blanket, wrapping around her warm, curvy body like he had so many times in his dreams. The circular skirt of the sundress was just large enough to keep all but their legs off of the sand. She'd drifted off within minutes of lying down, peaceful with no ghosts from the past haunting her.

He was haunted, though. Eventually, he'd have to face Walter. With the influence Gen's brother held over her, she might decide being with him wasn't worth it. A lump of dread rose in his throat. No. Hopefully, she was ready now. Moving out had been a big step for her, but he wasn't sure she was prepared to go the whole distance and stand up against her brother. Even if she were, it wasn't a given he'd ever approve of Chance.

Maybe he should have cleared things up all those years ago. Perhaps he wouldn't look so poorly on him now.

His current relationship with Walter was pretty much driven by past loyalty. Every time they met up, there was a stiff, distrusting air—like Walter wanted to believe what he knew in his heart about Chance from their childhood, but couldn't get past the rumors. He'd thought Walter would have worked through that by now, would have looked inside himself to discover the truth.

Something bit his leg and he rubbed his other foot over it. Yeah, he probably should have cleared things up that night. His relationship with Walter would probably be much different.

Again, something stung his calf and he brushed it off with his foot, not wanting to wake the woman in his arms.

Hopefully, Walter would be reasonable when he found out Chance had broken his promise to stay away from Genny, and not act like he had a decade ago. Surely it wouldn't get out of hand like that. They were all grown-ups, right? A sickening churn roiled his stomach. He hadn't kept his word. Just like his Dad.

No. This was not like his dad. He'd broken a promise, yes, but not at someone else's expense. It was just the opposite. The promise had hurt someone else. Breaking it was the right thing to do for Genny—and for him, too.

Gen rolled in his arms and made a frustrated huff, then kicked her legs before settling back into deep sleep. He propped up on an elbow and almost pinched himself. With her dark hair splayed over the fabric of the dress and one arm thrown over her head, she looked like a dream. The other arm rested across her flat belly, rising and falling in time with her relaxed breathing. And then there were those breasts. Perfect. Even better than he'd imagined after seeing her in that red dress seven years ago.

He ran his fingertips over her ribs, through her cleavage, and back down again, fascinated by her body's immediate response. Even in her sleep, her nipples hardened at his touch. He traced a wide circle around one breast and she smiled, still not fully awake. As he spiraled his path tighter, smoothing over her areola in a gentle circle, her eyes fluttered open and her breath caught. Then she grinned.

This. He could do this forever. But he had to be careful. He needed to talk to Walter before he took this to the next level. It was best for both of their sakes to not have sex until she cleared the air with her brother and was ready to be her own person at last.

He could wait. She was worth it.

"Mmmmm." She rolled to face him and put her hands on his face.

Waiting didn't mean they couldn't have fun until then, though. He reached for her, and she sat bolt upright, jerking out of his grip.

"Ouch!" She scratched her leg, then her shoulder. "Something bit me." She jumped to her feet. "Really bit me."

And then he was stung again. *Shit.* He'd totally underestimated the fucking insects. They were a nightmare some times of year, but he figured they wouldn't be a problem right now. Plus, he'd been distracted. Bugs were the last things on his mind.

"Here." He took her hand. "Our cottage is just a short distance away."

He gathered their clothes. After a quick run through the sand, which might have been his favorite part of the trip, they made it to the porch. Watching her run naked in the moonlight was going to be a hard act to top. Though as passionate as she'd proven herself to be, she could probably pull off a winner.

With that thought causing his dick to throb, he led her though the door, not even bothering to flip on the light. He knew every cottage on the island like the back of his hand. Like he wanted to know her body.

"Were those mosquitos?"

"The locals call them no-see-ums." He started the

shower. "Kind of like gnat-sized mosquitoes. Some times of year they're terrible. Fortunately, this isn't their high season."

"Thank goodness."

"How bad are your bites?" He tested the water and found it warm.

"Can't you tell by looking?"

He pulled two towels out of the cabinet and hung them over the bar near the walk-in shower. "The lights are off."

"Oh… They're not so bad. Some on my legs. One on my backside, I think."

He pulled her into the shower separated from the rest of the bathroom by a short wall. Along the back, there was a built-in bench, barely visible in the moonlight creeping in from the high window.

"Let me see." He turned her around, back to him.

"I thought the lights were off," she said over her shoulder.

"I want to look at you in *your* way." He ran his fingers from her shoulder blades, down to her middle back, but before he could get lower, she turned and caught his hands.

"Nuh-uh. If you're going to do this my way, really do it." She felt her way up his chest and looped her fingers under the strip of spandex still around his neck. He'd forgotten about the blindfold completely. "Put it on," she ordered.

And here he'd thought the run through the sand was the sexiest thing ever. He slid it over his eyes while she followed his actions with her fingers, checking to see it was firmly in place.

She turned her back to him. "As you were."

"Where was I?"

She giggled as he pretended to be totally confused, bumping his palms into the walls and then reaching around to grope her breasts, acting like he didn't have a clue what he had in his hands. She squealed when he gave her breasts a squeeze, then he pulled her back against him in the warm water. Her ass pressed against his dick and made him groan. "Gen..."

"Did you figure out which end was up yet?" she teased.

"I'll show you what's up." He nudged her from behind and she gasped, then turned to face him.

"Is there any soap?"

He patted the wall to his right and found the bar of soap, then handed it to her.

For the first time, he was tempted to cheat and adjust the blindfold so he could peek under it to watch her. Not knowing what she was doing was maddening, and honestly, exciting beyond words. Was she washing herself? Was she...? He hissed a breath through his teeth as she took him in her soapy hands. Well, that answered that.

"Shit, Gen." He braced himself on the wall as she stroked up and down, her soapy hand sliding easily over his hardened flesh. "Yeah. That's..."

And she stopped, just like that.

"What?"

"Shhhh."

He turned his head to hear her over the shower spray. She fumbled with something on the ledge—maybe putting the soap back.

"Is the stuff in the bottle shampoo?"

"It is."

"Turn around."

"Bossy woman."

"You like it."

"I do. Not gonna lie."

She smeared shampoo on his head and scrubbed in circles, her nails gently raking his scalp as warm water sprayed their bodies. No one had ever washed his hair before, and it felt amazing, sending tingles from his scalp all the way to his fingertips.

"Hand out," she ordered. He complied, and she filled his palm with liquid. "Your turn to shampoo my hair."

He knew that she came to about his shoulder, so he accurately located the sides of her head on the first try, spreading the shampoo to the ends, then massaging. She groaned and he grinned, loving her enthusiasm.

She then handed him the bar of soap.

"What's this for?"

"Claire's right. You and your brother are cavemen. It's for washing, Chance."

He scrubbed himself down as she followed his progress with an occasional touch. He removed the blindfold long enough to wash his face before she insisted he put it back on.

"Caveman clean." He thumped his fist to his chest. "Now, me show you how caveman washes woman."

She giggled.

He started with a leisurely scrub of her neck, and by the time he'd worked his way down her body to her feet and rinsed her, she was thoroughly clean, two orgasms richer, and slumped onto the built-in bench of the shower, panting. Pleased with himself, he stepped under the shower spray and rinsed. The knobs squeaked as he shut off the water, and cool air replaced the hot spray.

He reached in the direction of the towel bar, but was stopped short as she blocked his arm. "Let me show you how a woman thanks her caveman for washing her." She turned the water back on and his skin warmed again.

He wanted to rip off the blindfold. To watch her while she said sexy things like that. And—she pulled him to her by the hips—and see her when she did sexy things, too.

"You're not peeking, are you?"

"No." But he wanted to. His fingers itched to remove the fucking thing.

He groaned as her breath fanned across the skin of his

penis. Sitting on the bench in the shower, she was at just the right height to—

She flicked her tongue over his skin.

—do *that*. "God, Gen."

"Yeah?"

"Hell, yeah." His head fell back as she circled the head with her tongue, and he groaned again when she took him partway in her mouth. "I need to see you."

She pulled him from her mouth with a *pop*. "Nope. Forget it. Go with the senses you have. Focus on sounds. Let your ears see."

Torture. It was sheer torture not knowing when or where she'd touch him next. From her mouth on his shaft to her hands cupping his balls, every touch seemed new and unexpected. And to think this was how she experienced the world all the time.

When she set a rhythm with her hand in time to her mouth, he felt that familiar tightening of his balls and the low tingles in his back.

Then, as he braced his arms on the wall over her head to keep from losing his balance, she took him deeper in her throat and made a sound that vibrated from her mouth through his whole body. "Ah, shit."

It was all he could do to not thrust into her mouth. She made him wild. And happy. He couldn't recall a time in his adult life when he'd felt this free. "Gen," he said as she pulled back and then took him deeper. "My sweet Genny."

She moaned in her throat again, and he gritted his teeth, wanting more than ever to rip off the fucking blindfold and watch her. Instead, he focused on using his ears, like she'd suggested. The hiss of the water as it came through the showerhead and the way the drops splattered on the tile. The gurgle of the drain. The sensual, wet sounds of her taking him in and out of her mouth. The rasp of his own harsh breathing and the hammering of his heartbeat pounding in his ears.

All of these noises combined made a symphony so erotic, it took him right to that edge. "I'm gonna... Gen. I'm..."

"Mmmmhmmm."

And that was permission enough. His orgasm raged and he fought to remain standing. "Gen, Gen, Gen," he chanted until the spasms subsided, leaving him weak-kneed and light-headed.

And still the water cascaded to the tile with a hiss, and the drain gurgled, and eventually his heart no longer pounded like a jackhammer in his ears. "Oh, Gen." His breathing slowed and he could finally stand upright without the aid of the wall.

"Is the caveman happy?" she asked, rising to her feet, then reaching up to touch the blindfold.

"Happy?" He took her in his arms. "Ecstatic." She removed the blindfold, but he kept his eyes closed, loving the feel of her. "Fucking amazing."

"Me, too."

She tucked her head against his chest while the warm shower rained down on them as if washing away the rest of the world. Only, he knew that when this amazing week was over, the rest of the world would still be there, like it always had been. And right at the forefront would be Walter. Until they got past that hurdle, nothing was certain. As much as he'd like to pretend this little fantasy bubble were reality, he knew better. They needed to come up with a plan.

"So tell me about the wedding," Gen said, slipping into a comfy bathrobe she'd packed at Claire's house. She pulled a toothbrush from the bag and turned on the sink.

"This is sort of the warm-up act," Chance answered from

somewhere outside the bathroom. "They're getting married in a private wedding with no one attending but their very best friends, but in order to make Mom happy, they're having a huge blowout reception next month at the Waldorf Astoria, where she and dad had their wedding."

"Yeah. I knew about the party next month. My family received an invite and I thought it was weird the wedding was private." She dipped the toothbrush in the stream of water, coated it with toothpaste, and set to brushing.

The air stirred, and she knew he was back in the bathroom with her. "It was a compromise. Mom would have dragged the planning out forever, making everyone miserable, and Will and Claire wanted a ceremony right away. When they found out churches were all booked up for over a year, sometimes two, they decided to have the ceremony here on the island and let Mom do whatever she wanted for the celebration afterward."

She rinsed the toothpaste out of her mouth and cut off the water. "Yeah, your parents are always up for a big party. I especially loved the ones at your house over the holidays because of the chocolate fountain."

"Well, Mom's not happy about this at all, but the deal was, she stayed out of the wedding planning, and Mia and Claire and my brothers would let her have her way with the post-wedding party. Needless to say, it's going to be a blowout with a who's-who list a mile long. I'm sure Michael will be happy with the PR opportunity for the company, and Will is used to that kind of scene."

She leaned her hip against the counter as he turned the water back on and then brushed his teeth. It struck her as odd how comfortable she felt with this little domestic tooth-brushing moment—something completely foreign, but so natural with him. "You're different from your brothers."

"We're all different in our own ways. I'm far more

private. Probably because of what happened at the harbor. It's easiest to keep your head down when people are looking for the worst in you. My brothers have always been good with attention—not me."

"Doesn't it bother you to always stand in their shadows?" Like she had stood in Walter's her entire life.

"I don't feel overshadowed. They'd be the first ones to shine the spotlight on me if I'd let them, but I don't need all that. I've never wanted to be the powerful businessman. I don't want to be the war hero. I don't want any of that."

She felt like they were hovering on the edge. Skirting something big. After a few moments he turned off the water, and she broke the silence. "So, if you don't want any of that, what do you want?"

There was enough of a pause before he spoke to make her squirm, repositioning against the tile countertop.

"You."

And with that one word, her heart expanded to the point it felt too big for her chest. She was living a dream she didn't want to end. Even in her vivid imagination, she hadn't created a scenario this amazing. This perfection would be marred by their return to real life and Walter. So she vowed to continue to make the most of it now.

Heat radiated from where he stood right in front of her. And her body hummed with need. She wanted him.

Now.

Right at that moment, before the world or Walter had a chance to take him away from her again.

She placed her hands on his ribs, then slid them around to his spine, loving the way his muscles tightened under her fingers.

"Gen, we need to talk," he said, not doing anything to stop her exploration.

"Then talk." She ran her hands up his bare torso and

fanned them out over his chest. Nothing was going to get in her way of living this moment to the fullest. She loved him. No more holding back. *Number ten, here I come.*

"We need to talk about how to handle Walter."

Her hands stilled on his chest. "Walter needs to fuck off."

"Agreed, but we—" He cut off as she leaned forward and ran her tongue up his sternum. "Uh, we..." She circled his nipple with her tongue. "Gen. Seriously."

"I'm listening." But she wasn't. She was running her hands all over his body, memorizing him. Loving his scent and freshly showered taste.

"I can't think while you touch me."

"Then stop thinking."

He took her wrists in his hands. "We have to talk."

"We will. Just not now. We're alone. Please, let's enjoy it. Walter's done enough damage, hasn't he?"

"We need to talk before we take this any further."

"What? Why?" It blew her mind he was hesitating. Never had she wanted anything like she wanted Chance Anderson. Her whole life had led to this one amazing moment, and for once, she was determined to take her life into her own hands. "Number ten, Chance. We've almost completed the bucket list. We can't take care of dancing in the rain because there hasn't been any, but we can take care of number ten right here and now."

She twisted her wrists with no results.

"This is about so much more than a single-minded pursuit of knocking off bucket list items, Gen."

She stilled, surprised by the intensity of his voice and his firm hold on her wrists. Of course it was. It was about finally consummating a love they'd both suppressed for way too long. "I know. It's about us."

"Yes, it is. And it's also about Walter."

She tried to yank her arms away, but his grip was too

firm. "Like I said earlier, Walter can fuck off. I'm tired of him being in my business all the time and treating me like I'm helpless."

"And what are you going to do about that?"

"I don't know yet. I'll figure something out."

His grip relaxed. "Your family doesn't like me. They might never approve of us."

"I don't care." She pulled her hands free with no resistance.

"You say that now, but you're not thinking clearly. Neither of us is." He brushed her cheek and she pulled away from his touch. "We should wait until we are."

She couldn't believe it. He was going to pull the plug. Hand on bathroom counter for support, she took several steps away. "Are you serious? We've had our hands and mouths all over each other's bodies and you're saying we should wait? For what? For Walter's permission?"

"Yes. We should probably—"

Furious, she cut him off. "Fuck Walter! No... No, better than that, let's go from figurative to literal. Fuck *me*. Yeah. That's exactly what you should do because you want to and I want you to. Fuck me, Chance." Useless tears from equally useless eyes traversed her cheeks, and she wiped them away with the back of her hand. "Knock number ten off that list like I've dreamed about for a decade now."

"This is not simply a means to an end—another task to mark off. This is...it's..." His voice trailed off, and she reached forward, only finding empty space. He must have backed up as well.

She dropped her hand to her side. "When I wrote that list, I had no one else in mind but you. I still don't. I want you more than anything I've ever wanted in my entire life, and I know you feel the same way."

"The timing's not right."

"I know what this is," she said, taking a step closer. "You're only freaked out because you'll be my first. If that weren't the case, we wouldn't be having this conversation."

His silence confirmed she was right. She grabbed the handles of the bag on the counter, planning to go...she didn't know where. She had no clue as to the layout of the house. She slammed the bag down, defeated by her own deficiency.

Why? Why did she have to be like this? Why couldn't she have been sighted like everyone else? Being blind didn't make her special like Chance had told her. It made her off-limits. And she hated it. But most of all, she hated Walter, who had not only deprived her of Chance for ten years, he'd deprived her of this moment as well, his invisible presence looming over them like a specter.

She reached in the bag to pull out her cane and was stopped by a gentle hand over hers. She stilled, feeling like the pet rabbit she used to have whose heart beat a million times a minute when she held it.

"Gen." His voice was calming, and she loosened her grip on the folded cane. "Genny." He placed his hands on either side of her face. "I'm not holding back because I'd be your first." His lips brushed hers, and she took a deep, shuddering breath. He smoothed her bangs out of her face. "I'm holding back because I want to be your last."

Chapter Nineteen

Gen knew Chance was sincere, but he was wrong about waiting, and she intended to prove it. She barely listened as he described the room for her. "It's a small one-room cottage with a kitchen at three o'clock, living area straight ahead, and bed at nine o'clock." Well, the word "bed" caught her attention, anyway.

"The room is about twenty by twenty feet," he continued. "The bathroom is at noon from here, straight at the back. There's a two-person sofa dead center of the clock." After some rustling, she heard her cane snap as he assembled it.

"I could have done that."

"Of course you could have. It was a courtesy, like opening the door for you."

Like telling my brother before we have sex. She took the cane from him. "Thanks."

"Gen, don't think for one minute I'm not aware of your capabilities. You amaze me. You navigate the city—hell, you navigate the Times Square area, the worst possible part of the city to walk though imaginable, in my opinion—with less trouble than sighted people."

"I have a ton of help from my phone apps and assistive technology."

"You could do it without that."

He was right. She could. If only Walter could see that. Tapping across the tile floor, she found the sofa easily behind a low coffee table she knew was made of a dense wood from the sound of her cane against it.

She sat, aware her robe had fallen open because of the cool air over her skin. A halt in his footsteps toward her indicated Chance was aware her robe had gapped open as well. Maybe his resolve wasn't as strong as her desire.

Time to test that.

She slid her hands inside the robe and pulled it open fully, running her hands down her thighs.

"Gen…" His tone was full of warning, but she disregarded it, trailing her fingers back up her body in what she hoped would be a huge resolve-killer, pausing to circle her nipples.

"It's not going to work," he said, but the way his voice trailed off indicated otherwise.

"Don't tell me that. This works for me every time, Anderson." She continued the slow circles over her breasts, wishing it were his hands and not her own.

There were sounds of his bare feet on the tile and a frustrated huff. Then more footsteps, as he most likely paced the far side of the room. "Gen, I…"

"Shhhhh. Concentrating here."

"Jesus."

"You could always help me out, you know."

The footsteps resumed, and so did her display as she trailed her hands down her body and rested her head against the back of the sofa, eyes closed.

A growl issued from deep in his throat, and the pacing stopped.

"Mmmm," she said, not really feeling it now that she knew what it was like to have his hands where hers were.

"Fuck, fuck, fuck. Fuck me," he muttered.

"Okay."

"Stop it, Gen."

"No. You stop. We're grown-ass people. I shouldn't have to answer to my brother, and neither should you."

"Shouldn't..."

She slipped the robe off her shoulders and grabbed her cane. "Won't. Not anymore." She was unfamiliar with the room, but as attuned to him as she was to herself. Easily, she navigated the distance between them, cane lightly brushing his foot long after she had located him based on his scent and sounds alone. She let the handle of her cane go and it tipped to the floor with a sharp metallic *clang*. "Oops. I guess you'll have to lead me to the bed now."

He stood very still, but she could hear the tension in his breathing as his mind battled with his heart and body.

She was counting on his body winning the battle. "I know you want me. And I've wanted you since I understood what part went where."

Still he said nothing.

"Would you like me to show you where things go?"

He sucked in a breath through his nose. Close. She knew he was just about to cave.

"This." She reached out and ran her hand down his body to his impressive erection, running one finger up to the tip. "Goes..." She took the same finger and slipped it into her folds. "Here."

He made the sound between a moan and a pained whine. Then, he guided her finger into his mouth and it was her turn to moan as he circled her sensitive skin with his tongue. "Too much," he said. "You're too, too much."

"You say that like it's a bad thing."

"Bad in the best way possible." He picked her up, and her heart raced as she realized he was headed straight for nine o'clock—the bed.

Chance couldn't hold out any longer. He wanted her, she wanted him. Game over.

When she touched herself, the remaining shred of self-control exited his brain, right along with his reasoning as to why he was holding out in the first place.

He loved this woman. He always had.

After placing her on the bed, he stretched out beside her. In the moonlight, her luscious body appeared lit from within, and he grew even harder. "So, show me where things go again? I forgot."

She grinned and rolled toward him, reaching for his face, then tracing his dimples. "Well, first things first. Every girl knows to take precautions when engaging in this kind of activity."

"Sage advice." He trailed his hand up her side, and she squirmed. "Did you get that from one of the movies your friend narrates?"

"No. High school sex ed class."

"What kind of grades did you make in that class?" He reached into his bag by the side of the bed and then placed a packet in her palm, grateful his brother had slipped him supplies before they left his house, despite Chance's protest that he'd never break his promise.

"Straight As, of course."

"Of course." He ran his hand up her body, between her breasts, and lazily traced her lips with his fingers.

"What kind of grades did *you* make in that class?" she asked, nipping the end of his finger.

He drew his hand away and grinned at her feistiness. "I do much better in practical labs than the classroom setting."

"Show me."

He'd like to show her all right. Press her down into that mattress and let his body go, but this was not the time. She needed to lead and take it at her pace. "No. You said you'd show *me,* remember?"

"Oh, yeah." Her breath hitched a bit, and he was sure she was experiencing a small case of nerves. "About that…"

"Gen. I dare you to kiss me," he said, rolling her on top of him, positioning her legs to straddle his hips. "I dare you to kiss me like you've kissed me in your dreams. Pretend this is one of your movies and just do whatever feels right, because if it's good for you, believe me, it'll be great for me."

She smiled as her lips met his. The kiss was tentative at first, then more demanding as he ran his hands over her back. Soon, she'd lost herself in the kiss and her body naturally ground down against him, and he moaned. She pulled away and sat up, testing the feel of her body sliding against his, and she let her head drop back. He placed his hands on her hips and helped her set a rhythm.

As she slid back and forth along his cock, he imagined what it would be like to finally be inside her. Slick, hot… Genny.

"I need…"

She continued sliding over him as he cupped her breasts. "What do you need?"

"More."

He put his thumb between them and massaged her, and she quickened her pace.

Nothing was hotter than watching her grind against him reaching for a climax. "I dare you to come," he said. "Come hard, Gen, and then we'll take care of number ten on your list."

He bit his lip and fought back his own orgasm as she continued to pleasure herself on his body. Concentration lining her face, nipples hard as her breasts bounced with each grind. "Chance, I…"

"I'm here," he said. "Let go, Gen."

If she didn't come soon, number ten would have to wait a while. He'd go off and put them back at square one. She felt so right, though, sliding forward and back on top of him. Open and uninhibited. The perfect lover. His perfect love.

"Yes, Chance, I'm… Yes."

"I'm right here. Show me." Still circling her with his thumb, her tempo quickened and she gasped, then her legs tightened and she ground down harder. Finally, she called his name and he barely held on by a thread as her climax rocketed through her, leaving her limp and panting, draped over his body.

Once her head cleared, Gen sat up and reached for Chance's face. "You're frowning," she said, tracing the downward-turned lips.

"I'm concentrating."

"On?"

"Not ejaculating."

Oh… He was still impossibly hard beneath her, and a twinge of excitement zapped between her legs as she focused on his heat and shifted her weight.

"Don't move yet." He placed his hands on her thighs, and when she flattened her palms on his chest, his heart was beating hard and fast. "Please."

Weaving his finger through her hair, he pulled her down for a kiss. He tasted of toothpaste. She loved the way he kissed. Deep and focused, like he couldn't get enough of her.

And then he wrapped an arm around her waist and rolled her underneath him. Her legs fell to the sides, and she looped her arms around his neck, running her fingers through his hair.

"Now you're ready," he said. "And so am I."

Finally. Number ten. She ran her fingers up and down his spine, nails gently scraping, and his body bucked, causing a wet flush between her legs.

He kissed her neck and moved across to her shoulder, then down to her breast, where he swirled his tongue over her nipple, causing her to arch up against him. Then he moved to the other breast.

She moaned as he slid his fingers through her folds, then deep inside her. With an approving sound in the back of his throat, he withdrew his fingers. "So ready," he said, reaching for the packet still clutched tightly in her fist. He tore it open while she followed his actions with her fingers. Then he sat back on his heels between her thighs, as she traced his movements while he rolled on the condom.

Almost breathless, she waited. For years she'd waited, and now it was happening. And not just happening—it was happening with Chance.

He stretched over her, his warm, hard body covering hers, and she relaxed. He kissed her forehead, then her mouth, then her neck, and chills radiated from his lips down to her toes.

He propped himself up on his elbows, and his erection nudged right at her opening, hot and insistent.

"What do you see?" she asked.

"Only you." His voice was shaky, like he was overcome with emotion. "Aren't you going to ask me if I've done this before?"

She smiled, thinking back on how many times she'd asked him that question in their lives. "We both know you have."

He applied more pressure against her entrance, barely nudging inside, and she squirmed at the stretching sensation.

"But I haven't. Not like this." And farther still. "I've had sex, but I've never made love before." She relaxed the muscles that had tightened instinctively, and he gained another inch or so, pausing while her body adjusted to the intrusion. "You're my first. My first love. My only love."

The entire moment seemed surreal. She'd been in love with him her whole life, and now he was hers. It was more than their bodies joining. It was the past and present, and if she was very lucky, it was their future. "Chance..."

And then he thrust inside the rest of the way, leaving her breathless and him trembling. "Holy... Ah, Gen. So good." He placed his forehead against hers and pulled out almost all the way, leaving her feeling empty. He hovered over her, and she reached up to feel his face. Eyes closed, his mouth was drawn in a tight line as if concentrating. Then he slid back inside, and it was unlike anything she'd ever felt. Hard and hot, he stretched her and filled her until she had to move her hands to his back so she could get more of him. Putting her feet flat on the mattress, she pushed up to meet him, and he groaned, then pulled out again. She knew him well enough to know that's what was going on in his mind. He was going slow because he didn't want to hurt her, but it wasn't what either of them needed.

"More," she said, voice breathy and deep. "Stop holding back. I need more."

"God, Gen." He thrust again, harder this time, staying deep inside until she felt that familiar tightening in her body. "So good. You feel so good." And then he began thrusting for real, in and out, while she held on to his back. She moved her hands to his powerful backside, loving the feel of his muscles flexing as he worked.

Again and again he plunged, and she arched up to meet him, friction in just the right place with each stroke to bring her closer and closer to the edge again. Her body gripped his deep inside and he groaned, his chest rubbing over hers, sliding over her nipples and driving her wild as she lost track of where she ended and he began.

"Chance, I'm…"

"Gen. Genny. *Genny.*"

And with a groan, he thrust hard, body shaking, taking her right along with him, her back arching to get even more of him.

But she'd never get enough of him. As her body spasmed around his, it illustrated what she'd known for the last decade. They belonged together. They were a perfect fit in all ways, and no one, not even Walter, could keep them apart now.

Chapter Twenty

Gen awoke surprisingly rested for someone who'd spent all night making up for lost years. Chance had kept her on her toes...and knees and back and everything else, until they finally cried "uncle" and drifted off to sleep somewhere in the early morning hours.

She grinned and stretched when they made it down the porch steps into the soft sand, loving the general soreness all over and the specific soreness in certain places.

Turning toward the warmth of slanting morning sun, she sighed. A seabird screeched and the waves *shooshed* up on the shore in a relaxing tempo. *Heaven.* She wished they could stay on the island forever, but bliss would end Monday when she returned to her job...and the inevitable grilling she'd receive from her big brother once she turned her phone back on. She'd left it with Claire's on the plane when she was told there was limited to no reception on the island, and nobody used a phone here.

Dread pinched her throat for a moment at the thought of what was certain to be an epic lecture from her big brother, who called and checked up on her daily like she was an invalid. The real problem boiled down to the fact that he held all the cards financially. She made a good salary, but she still relied on drafts from her trust left by her grandparents. A trust he controlled, thanks to a power of attorney she'd signed at her parents' urging when she turned eighteen and the world still seemed dangerous and impossible to navigate. They were consumed with the notion she'd need someone to look out for her after they were gone, and since Walter was a lawyer, they thought it was a brilliant move. She hadn't, but went along with it in her usual compliant fashion.

She took a deep breath through her nose and pushed the anxiety down, focusing on the warm breeze on her face and the fresh sea air.

Chance twined his fingers through hers, and they struck out through the sand.

"I'm starving," he said. "We need to take provisions back to our cottage after the wedding so I can stay fueled up to keep up with you."

"I didn't hear you complaining last night."

"You sure didn't." He pulled her to a stop and wrapped his arms around her. Reaching up, she ran her hands through his shower-wet hair. "And you didn't hear me complain this morning, either." He kissed her, and her body roared to life. "Nor will I complain this afternoon when this wedding is over, nor tonight, nor tomorrow or any day after that."

Any day after that. The long-term reference made her feel buoyant, like she could fly. But then Walter's angry voice in her mind sent her plummeting back to earth. Tomorrow she'd return home. Back to the real world and her overbearing big brother. There had to be a way to get him to see reason and lighten up. To show him she was self-sufficient and didn't need an overseer.

"You okay?" he asked. Her face must have reflected her

thoughts.

"Yeah. You?"

"I'll be better when you're naked on top of me again," he said, nipping her earlobe. "Flat rude of my brothers to interrupt our day with a wedding."

They struck out again, and she was relieved there were no biting insects. No-see-ums. Her new spirit animal—or at least a good nickname.

The dress Claire had lent her for the wedding flowed around her legs, making her feel light and feminine. Beautiful, like Chance had described her over and over last night.

Pushing thoughts of Walter aside, she smiled and fell into step beside him, bare feet sinking in the soft, warm sand.

She heard voices before they made it to the porch of the main house. The low thrum of Will's baritone sax... then Claire's oboe. And there was someone else. A deep, masculine voice as well, but there was a harder edge to it. As they neared, she still couldn't make out words, but there were crisp consonants punctuating his speech. When they climbed the steps to the porch, the words sharpened into focus.

"Chance should take this up in private with him," the unfamiliar voice said.

"No. Gen needs to be a part of the conversation," Claire answered.

"I agree with Claire," Will said.

Chance paused on the porch, grip tightening on Gen's hand. His alarm was contagious, coiling like a snake up her arm, threatening to constrict and cut off circulation.

The unfamiliar voice spoke again. "I want to talk to Chance alone and let him make the choice. No need to stress out little sister. This is between Walter and Chance."

So much for pushing thoughts of Walter aside.

"You might be right, Michael," Will answered.

Oh shit. The new voice was Chance's big brother.

She'd met him only a few times as a child, but read about him regularly. The tabloids made him out to be powerful, ruthless, and untouchable. But observing Will and Chance together made her doubt that. How could he be so different from his brothers? And he was getting married along with Will. That didn't fit what she'd read about him being a man-whore, either.

"It's all good," Chance assured her. The hinge squeaked as he opened the door.

But it *wasn't* good. She could feel the tension in the air—sense it, not only through his touch, but in the silence that greeted them as they stopped inside.

"Michael. Good to see you. Happy wedding day." Subtle vibrations down his arm to their clasped fingers indicated he was shaking hands with his brother.

Something thumped to her right, possibly someone kicking a shoe off? She turned her head toward it. "Did you guys have a nice night, Gen?" Claire asked.

"Yes." Nice didn't even come close. She turned her head, trying to get a reading on the room. It was unusual for her to feel so disoriented. Not only was she unfamiliar with her surroundings, she didn't know where everyone was or what they were doing. She was aware this was the living area, but she'd only spent time in the kitchen, dining room, and porch so far.

"Where's Mia?" Chance asked.

"She's a little under the weather and is taking a nap with the dogs." He cleared his throat. "Listen, Chance, we need to talk. Do you have a minute so we can speak alone?" Well, true to the tabloids' description, Michael was direct, with no bullshit.

To her surprise, Chance's hold on her hand loosened. "Regarding?"

There was rustling from Michael's direction, then Chance

took a deep breath and let it out slowly. She tilted her head and turned her ear toward Michael to try to figure out what was happening.

"No need to speak alone," Chance said.

"I'd prefer it," Michael answered.

"I wouldn't."

Enough. "What's going on?" she demanded.

There was a long, tense pause, then a frustrated huff before Chance answered. "Michael just showed me a picture on his phone. You were right about the fountain. Someone got a picture of us."

Her stomach dropped like she was descending on a superfast elevator.

"It's..." He moved his hands to her shoulders. "It's obvious in the photo we're...good friends."

Good friends. The elevator hit the bottom before her stomach. She covered her mouth, not sure what bothered her most: his minimized description of their relationship or the fact that Walter might have seen a picture of them together.

"Good friends?" Michael said. "It looks like you're giving her a tonsillectomy with your tongue."

"Okay. So I lost my head and wasn't very discreet. You're a fine one to throw stones. Shall we talk about a kiss between you and Mia on Bow Bridge a while back?"

"This is different."

"Oh, because it's me and not you?"

"Be cool, little brother." Will's voice came from the back of the room, near the kitchen door. She had now placed everyone in the room.

Michael cleared his throat. "No. Because your secretary went through your office voicemail and you'd received a very angry phone call and some threats because of it."

Walter.

Chance guided her to a chair and put her hand on the arm

of it. His fingers trembled, and she wondered if it was fear like hers at being discovered, or anger. She sat, too numb to do much else. This couldn't be happening. For the first time in a decade, she'd felt free and happy. Now, her big brother was going to ruin everything...again.

"Walter called the office late yesterday evening looking for you when the photo came out attached to a column about Michael and Mia," Will said. "Mildred replayed the message for Michael when he got to the office early this morning."

"He's pissed, Chance. Really pissed," Michael said. "Evidently, when Will told him about the trip to the island, he mentioned Gen would be helping Claire, but he omitted the small detail that you would be here, too."

"Yeah, well," Will said, voice low. "That seemed unimportant to me at the time. It just slipped my mind."

"Of course it did. And he was really hot about the fact that her phone was off. Did that slip your mind, too?"

"Um, that was my suggestion," Claire said. "I told Gen to give her regular life a rest and leave her phone on the plane like I do."

Shit, shit, shit, this was bad. Walter would keep her on such a tight leash now, she'd never be out from under his thumb. God, he'd probably tell her she had to move back home with her parents again. *No. Freaking. Way.*

There were footsteps at the far end of the room, like when Chance paced last night. Bare feet padding across tile, followed by his voice. "You said he made threats. What did he threaten?"

Michael answered from farther away this time, perhaps by the kitchen door.

"Most of it was blowing off steam. He threatened everything from legal action for kidnapping, to physical violence, to flying out here to take her back home."

Take her back home. Back to her safe life. Safe... *Yeah,*

pass the mints, please. When would Walter understand she was grown? She was self-sufficient and could make her own choices, including who she… She took a deep breath. Who she knocked number ten off her bucket list with.

"Gen and I will talk this out and deal with it however she wishes," Chance said.

"I'm so sorry." Gen cringed inwardly. It figures an apology would be the first words out of her mouth. She seemed to spend her life apologizing. "I am sick this is interfering with your wedding. The last thing I want is to ruin—"

A hand on her shoulder cut her off. Roses. It was Claire. "Gen, we're getting married in a few hours no matter what happens with your brother. We're in love and happy. Nothing can ruin our wedding." Claire's voice shifted from above her head to her right side. She'd probably knelt by her chair. "What we want is for you two to be happy. Don't spare a thought for us. Think of you."

Will added, "Try not to fret it, Gen. We're all behind you in this. I'll give Walter a call and calm him down. He'll be civil because he wants to do business with Anderson Enterprises. Enjoy your last two days here, and when you get home, you and Chance can go talk some reason into him and end this once and for all. Until then, make yourselves useful and help us take the dishes and silverware to the tent outside."

Chance's familiar scent met her nose as he wrapped her in his arms, his warmth bolstering her like fuel. "I'm here. You've got this."

Staying busy helped, but Chance could still see the tension in every move Gen made. After the single large round table was set up and chairs in place, he and Gen arranged silverware while the brides and grooms got ready. The minister arrived and turned out to be their youth leader at church when they were in high school, so he caught them up on all their classmates, and to his credit, he didn't mention Chance's spotty past.

Before long, the bride's friends arrived, in matching free-flowing sundresses, and soon after that, Chance found himself standing barefoot in the sand, filling the role of best man to both of his brothers. His red hibiscus Hawaiian shirt matched those of his brothers, and to everyone's amusement, Michael's dogs had on scarves made from the same material.

They'd been through a lot, the three of them, and he was proud and happy for his brothers, but also, as he stood there, listening to them exchange vows with the women they loved, he found himself uneasy. Would he ever have this moment?

During the ring exchange, he peeked over his shoulder. Genny sat in the only row of chairs next to Mia's maid of honor's husband, Mark, and the two dogs. When Claire said the wedding would be small, she wasn't kidding. Not even a photographer other than Mark, who was snapping off shots on his phone.

Gen had her face turned toward the beach wind, rather than the wedding. Perhaps she could hear better that way, or maybe, like him, her thoughts were elsewhere. Maybe on how she'd handle the situation with her brother. As much as he'd like to take Walter on himself or face him side by side with Gen, this was her battle to fight. If she wanted to become independent, she'd need to act independently; otherwise, she was using one crutch to displace another. He wouldn't, couldn't be that crutch. Hopefully this time, she was ready to stand up for herself. Until she was, his role in life might be no more than this: to bear witness to other people's happiness.

Gen shoved her fish around on her plate with her fork, not able to take a bite. The thought of confronting her brother, and the fact that he'd threatened the Andersons, turned her stomach. Every now and then, Chance would touch her under the table; he was as distracted as she was. Still, she'd grown to love these people, and she needed to put on a good face, regardless of the fact that her big brother loomed over her happiness like a threatening storm cloud. Not only could he make her miserable, he could deny payments from her trust for her apartment rent, which would mean moving back home with her parents. Someday, she'd have enough from salary alone, but living in the city was expensive, so for the next few years, she needed that trust money, which meant she needed Walter.

Michael's bride, Mia, seated to her left, was not eating either. She could tell because she hadn't moved at all. Nor was she engaged in the animated discussion of a Greek archaeological dig between Claire and Michael. On her right, Will, and Mia's friends, Mark and Sue, laughed about something Michael did during their wedding in the Hamptons recently.

"You okay?" Michael whispered to his new wife.

"Yeah. More of the same."

"Now's as good a time as any."

"Do it," she said.

A high, staccato rapping of metal on glass silenced the table. "I have an announcement to make," Michael said.

"You've decided to stop being a controlling ass?" Laughter followed Will's joke.

"No," Mia said. "That will never change." More laughter.

"Mia and I..." He seemed to honestly be choked up. Gen turned her head to hear the rest of the table, which had fallen silent. Nothing moved except the sea breeze ruffling the curtains on the tent.

"Michael knocked me up!" Mia said.

Claire squealed and Mia laughed.

"Holy, shit, Mikey!" Will said. "You're shooting live bullets. Who'd have thought it?"

The table erupted in excited conversation and slaps on the back.

Chance's warm hand covered hers under the table and he squeezed her fingers.

In the midst of the celebration, a familiar buzz met her ears.

No. Surely it was just a passing boat. Walter had threatened to come get her, but he wouldn't do something that obnoxious, would he? It would take a total asshole to interrupt a wedding.

The boat motor got louder, and she stiffened. Walter was an asshole. Everything in her knew it wasn't a passing boat. It was her brother coming to take her away.

"Hey. You okay?" Chance ran his hand over her knee under the table.

No. She was not okay. She may never be okay again. "Yeah, I just…" She turned her head to listen, and his hand tightened. He wasn't breathing. It was Walter.

"Visitor, Chance," Will said. "Would you mind meeting him at the dock rather than letting him embarrass himself up here?"

"Not at all."

"Oh, God. I'm so sorry about this, Will. I…"

And then she noticed the table had fallen silent. Walter had ruined everything. The wedding, the news of Michael and Mia's baby… Now everyone would see her as the helpless, disabled child her brother saw. "I'm sorry."

Gen got to her feet, wishing she had her cane. Not because she needed it with Chance to assist her, but it made her more secure. As a little girl, when Walter would chew her out, she'd imagine herself smacking him over the head with it. Maybe it was a good thing she didn't have it after all. She might skewer him with it and screw up the wedding even more than she had already.

"Well, I guess it's showtime," Chance said, slipping his hand into hers. "Ready?"

"Yes." *No.* She'd never be ready. Her brother was coming to take her away.

Again.

The panic of the night in the harbor didn't hold a candle to this. Her freedom was being ripped out from under her again. And short of causing a huge scene, which she refused to do, there was no stopping it. This was supposed to be the happiest day of his brothers' lives, and she was turning it into a fiasco.

Instead of the sunshine blanketing her in comfort and hope like it had earlier, it felt like a hot spotlight shining on all her flaws as she stepped from under the tent's shade.

"It'll work out," Chance said. "We'll get through this."

Chance was her knight in shining armor, ready to do battle against the dragon and free her from her prison. If only it were that simple.

Chapter Twenty-One

Chance squinted in the sunlight as they neared the pier. A boat made its way toward them, bow lifted as it skimmed over the water.

He thought of how brave Gen had been when driving the boat. Would she be that brave again today, flying into the unknown based on trust alone? A glance at her troubled expression had him betting against it.

He'd thought she was ready, but perhaps she still needed more time. His heart ached at the prospect that she'd let her brother keep the upper hand—that she'd choose to go back to her sheltered life, rather than take a stand for herself. For *them*.

Everything in him wanted to confront her brother and make this right for her, but if he stood up to Walter, rather than allowing her to do it, he would simply be stepping into her brother's shoes as a crutch. He knew now that he wasn't dangerous for her, but he could be her conduit to freedom only if she threw open her own cage door.

"I'm sorry about this," she said again. Like the times

before, he simply squeezed her hand. This was not his decision to make. He did intend to make sure Walter was in control before he allowed him access to Gen, though.

He stopped halfway down the narrow pier and placed Gen's hand on a piling. "I'll talk to him, and then the rest is up to you."

She released his hand, holding tight to the piling. "This is bad, isn't it?"

"Only if we let it be." His words were more confident than his tone. *Only if* you *let it be.*

She turned her head with a jerk, and he knew she'd heard something other than the single motor on the small boat in the distance. And then he heard it, too. Walter was shouting his name like a curse.

As if she were trying to keep her heart from leaping out, she pressed her hand over her chest. "Oh God."

He smoothed her hair over her shoulder. "You've got this."

The boat was now close enough to make out Walter's drawn face. Chance's body readied instinctually, just as it had thousands of times over the last ten years before taking a strike. "Hell hath no fury like a brother scorned," he said under his breath.

"That's not the quote." Her voice cracked, and his chest ached at her fear.

Be strong, Genny, he willed her silently, gently kissing her. *And please understand what I'm doing and why.*

Walter's face was red, but Chance doubted it was from the sun. While Gen clutched the piling, he took several steps forward, fully aware of his brothers at the base of the pier. They had his back, as expected.

Just like before every match, his senses heightened—not to Gen's level, of course, but the fight-or-flight instinct kicked in, readying him. Only this time, he wouldn't give his body over to instinct. It was imperative he stay in control, because in the end, it wasn't his battle to fight, but hers.

"You fucking bastard," Walter shouted, throwing a rope over a piling at the end of the pier. "You promised to stay away from her after you almost killed her." He stepped up onto the pier and charged. "You promised you'd never touch her, and you did." He threw a punch, but Chance deflected it with his forearm, easily throwing Walter's momentum to the side and almost landing him in the water. After catching his balance, Walter came with another punch, this time from the left hand, and Chance caught his fist. His onetime friend froze, evidently grasping that Chance had a firm advantage.

Gaze locked on his friend's angry blue eyes, Chance released the fist, and Walter wisely took a step back.

"You fucking lying asshole," Walter said, rubbing his fist.

Chance's muscles relaxed slightly. "Yes."

"You're not good enough for her. You're a loser. She's... she's..."

"Yes, she's blind. I know."

"Do you? Do you know exactly what that means?"

"I believe so."

Walter pointed to where his sister hugged the piling. Her entire demeanor had changed back into that hurt little girl on the bleachers all those years ago, and Chance wanted nothing more than to take her in his arms.

"She's not able to take care of herself," Walter said. "How can you take care of her when you have so many issues of your own?"

"That's an excellent question."

"You smart-ass son of a bitch." Walter raised his fists and took a step forward, but dropped his arms to his side when Chance did nothing but arch a questioning eyebrow and brace his feet wider.

A quick glance over his shoulder confirmed Gen was

at the piling and his brothers stood at the ready back at the steps. He turned his attention fully on Walter again.

"This girl needs a full-time caretaker for the rest of her life. She can't even handle funds because she can't see the money. She has to be watched because she could get snatched up or lost at any time." His gaze fell on his sister, and his expression soured as if he'd eaten a bug.

Chance said nothing, but from the corner of his eye, he saw the look of horror on Gen's face. It was an expression similar to the one she wore a decade ago in the hospital. Like then, she said nothing. And for a fleeting moment, he thought he might vomit.

Gen dug her nails into the side of the piling, stunned.

Chance loved her. She knew he did, yet, like ten years ago, there he was, not standing up for her or defending her at all.

This couldn't be happening.

She tried to think back on what he'd told her about that night. That he'd not defended himself or her because it would have made no difference.

But it would make a difference now. Instead of defeating the dragon, he was enabling it to take her away.

It wasn't really his battle though, was it? It was up to her to face Walter. To finally stand up for herself. Still, his silence stung.

She thought about how Will had told her she could find her way on the beach with no assistance. How Claire had treated her like a normal person. How Chance had made her feel beautiful and alive.

"Come on, Gen," Walter said. Heavy footsteps neared and the vibrations from them became more distinct the closer he came. "Let's go home."

But most of all, she realized how Walter made her feel. Small, helpless, disabled. She needed to break away from this.

Her brother's familiar hand wrapped around hers as music started up from the tent on the beach.

She turned her face toward Chance, but picked up nothing.

Stumbling behind as her brother led her over the wooden planks, she stopped short, pulling him to a halt. Like before, she was devastated by Chance's silence, but this time was different. This time, she wouldn't let her brother destroy her. She wouldn't put up the fight she wanted to and ruin the wedding, but she would not be dragged off like a naughty child, either.

"Let me go, Walter. You've barged into a wedding, did you know that? Will and Michael Anderson just got married and you screwed it all up."

There was a silence that indicated he didn't know the wedding was happening at that time. "No. You screwed it up by coming here with that loser," he answered, taking her arm again.

She pulled away. "I'm coming with you, Walter, but not because you scare me or because I have even a tiny spark of respect for you. I'm coming because the Andersons don't deserve to have their wedding day ruined, and you and I need to talk."

Turning her head, she heard Chance's breaths over the sea wind. "I…" She didn't even have the ability to form words. Together, they could have convinced Walter to go away. Her heart felt like it was shattering. Once again, he'd remained silent during her brother's rant. She knew he loved her. He'd said he wanted her forever. *I know myself well enough to know when to step back or step up,* he'd said only yesterday.

Her confusion must have shown on her face, because

Chance moved closer and spoke in a low, even voice. Almost like it was an emotionless recording. "You don't need a caretaker. No cane clearing your way. No brother propping you up. No lover distracting you. Freedom you earn is more powerful than freedom handed to you."

And then he did the most confusing thing of all—he helped her into the boat with her brother.

The motor revved to life, and barely over the rumble, she heard Chance's voice.

"I'm sorry, Genny."

Chapter Twenty-Two

Chance didn't move until he could no longer see the boat on the horizon, then he sat at the end of the pier, legs dangling into the water, like he'd done as a boy. If only things could be simple like they were back then. Like they'd been last night. Just him and Gen with nothing else in the way.

Will joined him on the end of the pier, feet hitting the water with a splash. "You let her go."

A waterbird landed on the surface a few yards out, then took off with something in its beak, water spraying from its wings. "I had no choice."

"Like hell you didn't. You've seriously got the most fucked-up logic, little brother."

Maybe he did. "When you love someone, you have to let her go."

"When you love someone, you fight for her."

"Now you're the one with the fucked-up logic, big brother. You can only fight for someone who is willing to fight for herself."

Will studied his toes beneath the surface of the clear

water and scrubbed a hand over his closely cropped head. "It scares me that that makes sense."

Far overhead, a gull rode the air currents, wings motionless. "It would have been so much easier to lay Walter out," Chance said.

"You would never have done that."

"I wouldn't have. You're right. But I wanted to."

His brother grinned. "It would have been fun to watch."

"It would have been fun to do." His brother laughed, and Chance took a deep breath of clean sea air through his nose. "I wanted to tell him off. Really let him know how wrong he was about her, but that's not my battle to fight. It would only have been a short-term solution to a long-term problem. She would have been substituting one crutch for another. Me for him. She needs to stand on her own first. Besides, it would mean nothing to Walter coming from me."

"But it would mean something to her. Have you ever considered that she needs to hear it? To know you've got her back?"

He stared at his brother, not really even seeing his face. "If she doesn't know that, she never will. She made her choice." And deep inside, in that place only she could reach, the pain was almost unbearable.

They sat in silence, side by side, while the waves lapped the pilings. "So, what are you going to do now?" Will asked.

He rose to his feet. "Celebrate my new sisters-in-law and tease the shit out of Michael about being a dad."

"We'd all understand if you wanted to go after Gen, Chance. Don't stick around here because of us."

"If I thought going after her would benefit the end game, I'd swim all the way there right now with an arm tied behind my back. But going after her won't solve the real problem. Only she can."

"Does she know that? Because she looked like you'd

dumped her when she left."

"God, I hope she does." If not, he'd just made the biggest fuckup in the history of fuckups.

Sherry grabbed another handful of popcorn and muted the end credit music—if it could be called music. It was like a 1970s synthesized calliope. "Pass the bag of chips. It's right in front of you on the coffee table."

Gen sighed and passed the chips. It had been two days since her silent trip back with Walter, and she hadn't spoken to anyone except Sherry since her return.

"Okay. Time for a chat. If watching smut doesn't cheer you up, you're in deep need of girl talk." The chip bag crinkled as she grabbed a handful. "I saw your brother drop you off Saturday. Did you tell him to fuck himself, finally? You've wanted to since I met you."

"He wouldn't talk to me in the boat on the way back, and he bought plane tickets on opposite ends of the cabin, probably to avoid me. When I tried to talk to him in the car, he told me he'd wasted enough time coming to fetch me and then put his headphones in and made business calls."

"Sounds like you're making excuses to avoid conflict as usual."

"I don't avoid..." Okay, maybe she did. Old habits were hard to break. And then she thought of Chance and what he'd been through. His habits had been a hell of a lot harder to break than her codependence on her big brother.

It was Monday. He must have gotten back last night. *I'm sorry, Genny*, he'd said...right before he helped her into the boat.

Reaching over, she found the bag of chips in her friend's lap and grabbed a few. Did he ache like she did? He was probably at his gym, or whatever it was called, working those delicious hard muscles and making shouting sounds. She shoved some chips in her mouth and shifted on the sofa.

"I'd really love some more details about the island trip."

"We've been through this. We met, we played, we kissed, we banged, we came, I left."

"Oooh. Not only funny, but worthy of a line in that movie we just finished. Cut the act. You and I both know there's a lot more going on here than a bang."

"You're right. Four bangs… Maybe five. It was a busy night. I lost count."

"You're hilarious." The dry tone in her voice let Gen know she'd gone too far.

"So I'm told."

The chip bag crinkled as Sherry grabbed a handful. "What are you going to do?"

Gen shifted in the sofa to face her friend. "I don't know."

"Have you thought about calling him?"

"I want to."

"But?"

"But, dammit, he did the exact same thing again. He let Walter call me helpless and he didn't defend me. And then, Walter called him a loser and said he wasn't good enough for me, and he just *took* it."

Sherry was quiet a long time. Not even chips or popcorn crunching, which had been constant since the movie began. "Did you defend *him*?"

"No. He can defend himself."

"So, let's see if I got this straight. People who can see must defend those who can't, because blind people are unable to speak for themselves or others." The crunching resumed.

"What? Wait. No! That's ridiculous."

"Then why didn't you speak up? You're no different than he is. You're not that little girl your big brother has to look out for and control." The chip bag rustled. "Or are you?"

"Of course I'm not."

"Then stop acting like it."

Gen traced the entry keypad with her fingers and took a deep breath. She could navigate Grand Central in rush hour by herself. Comparatively, this meeting should be a piece of cake. But it wasn't. This was a lifetime of baggage to unpack.

Biting her lip, she entered the apartment number.

"Yes?"

Just the sound of his voice made her heart rate increase. "It's me, Walter. Buzz me in."

"Gen?"

"Yeah. Let me in."

The door lock clicked and she pushed it open. She'd never been to Walter's apartment before, but she knew he lived on the fifth floor. No doorman or desk, but her phone app identified the elevator easily when she double-tapped her screen. Before she could find the elevator call button, the door slid open with a ding. Old Spice deodorant wafted out.

"Hey, Walter."

"What are you doing wandering the streets this time of night? Holy shit, Gen. How—"

"Great to see you, as well, thanks. I'm glad I stopped by, too." She could feel him right in front of her, blocking the elevator, so she nudged past and felt for the buttons, relieved she hit the correct side with the panel on the first try, then elated when there were braille labels. She found and depressed the fifth-floor button before the door even closed.

His breathing was irregular, but she wasn't sure if he was mad or still surprised at her unannounced visit—her first, and possibly last visit to his apartment, depending on how this went. And it struck her, as they rose in silence, they were almost strangers. Not only had Chance withdrawn that horrible night ten years ago, so had her brother, reducing their roles to that of caretaker and cared-for.

The door slid open and she stepped out, waiting for him to lead the way.

"My place isn't handicapped accessible," he said, taking her elbow.

Of course that would be his first consideration. "Neither are you."

He stopped and opened a door. "What does that mean?"

She located the threshold with her cane and entered the apartment before he invited her in. "Exactly what you think it means. In your eyes, I'm handicapped. You're not accessible, hence, my surprise attack."

She tapped her phone screen and waited until the app identified a sofa. Using her cane, she made her way around a coffee table and sat while he remained by the door. Ordinarily, she would let the other person help her out because the app took longer, but she was making a point. She didn't need him or anyone.

The door closed with a *click*.

"Please sit down, Walter. This might take a while."

"I have work in the morning."

"So do I. And my job is no less important to me than yours is to you, but this is even more important."

There was a creak as he sat somewhere across the coffee table from her, and she swallowed the lump in her throat. All her life, she'd let her parents and brother take the lead and direct everything from conversations to schedules because it was easier—safer. Her time with Chance and his family had shown her the easy way wasn't always the best. And this long-overdue conversation certainly wasn't going to be easy.

She took a deep breath and began the way she'd practiced

with Sherry. "Now, I'm going to talk and you're going to listen, for once."

"How did you get here?"

"That's not listening. How do you think I got here? How do *you* get here?"

"I take the subway."

"That's how I got here."

"You got on a subway at night?"

"Four stops between us on a safe part of the line. Yes. But only because you ignored me the entire trip back from the island."

"I did not ignore you."

"I'm blind, not stupid. Give it a rest there, bro."

He was quiet for a while, which wasn't like him. She'd never talked to him this way before. Maybe her guns-blazing approach was effective, like Sherry said it would be.

"So, here's the deal, Walter. You're going to butt out of my life and start acting like a brother, not a jailer."

"All I've ever wanted is what's best for you."

"Great. We have the same goal then."

"Gen, listen—"

"No, *you* listen. I know you love me, Walter, and you're trying to do the right thing, but you're doing it all wrong. So are Mom and Dad." She placed her hands on her knees to keep from fidgeting. He needed to see her as she really was, not as he perceived her. It was essential she come across as mature and in control. "I'm not a little girl, and I'm not helpless. I can do lots of things you don't give me credit for. Take money, for instance. I use a debit card most of the time, but I can use cash because of the Tap Tap See app you saw me use when I came in. It identifies bills and coins easily. I have voice-over on every device I own, and I bet I can text and use a map app faster than you."

He said nothing, to her surprise.

"It's not like I'm a person who has relied on sight her whole life, suddenly blinded and having to navigate in a whole new way. I've always been like this. In fact, until I was four or so, I thought everyone was like me. It's all I've known."

He gave a sigh like he was enduring a child's tantrum. "I know that."

Angry prickles crept up her neck. "So you know what it's like, then? How frustrating it is when people yell at me because they think I'm deaf or talk to me like I'm two years old?"

Again, he used an indulgent tone. "I'm sure it's frustrating."

"It is. But you know what the most frustrating thing is? It's my own family treating me with more ignorance than complete strangers."

There was a rustle of fabric, like he'd crossed his legs or shifted in his chair. Good, she'd made him uncomfortable.

"I'm a full-grown woman with a career and goals, not an invalid."

"I know you're not an invalid. I allowed you to move out and get a job."

"You allowed me? *Allowed?*" Her anger and indignation flared, twisting her stomach in knots. "See, that's the problem. It's the allowing." She ran her hands through her hair. "I've allowed *you* to control my life, but I'm stopping that tonight."

Her proclamation was met with a long-suffering sigh that made her blood boil. "Gen. Mom, Dad, and I—"

"Stop! Just stop." She slapped her palm on the coffee table and something on top of the glass top rattled. "I'll no longer bow down to the holy trinity of sightedness. You guys have erected this wall between me and real life, and while I appreciate the fact that you think it's for my own good, it's not. You don't know me well enough to make decisions for me like this."

"That's nonsense. We know you better than anyone." His tone didn't have its flippant dismissiveness from before.

"What do I do for a living?" She sat back and crossed her arms over her chest.

"You work at a sound studio."

Now it was her turn to reply with a long-suffering sigh. "Doing what?"

"Something with recordings."

"I'm the head mixer for Decibels, one of the top studios on the East Coast. I specialize in orchestral balance. Like huge, symphonic recordings. I make sure all instruments are balanced and the piece is true to the conductor's vision. I've worked on operas, symphonies, Broadway cast recordings, and even rap. People request me by name because I'm good at what I do. Really good. Not in spite of the fact I'm blind, but *because* of it. Granted, it's not a big-bucks job yet, but in a few years, it will be. I plan to open my own sound studio someday."

He cleared his throat, but said nothing.

"What's my favorite food? My favorite band?"

There was silence from the other side of the table.

Leaning forward, she placed her palms flat on the cool glass of the coffee table. "You don't know, but you know who does? Chance knows. Because he sees me as a person, not a liability. I'm going to help you out here. I'm releasing you from your liability. I want complete control of my life, even if it means walking away from everything and starting over."

She sat back, hoping he had heard her finally. "You need to pull your head out of your ass and use those oh-so-superior eyes and take a look at me, Walter. You also need to look at Chance, who has suffered for ten years because of something that was a total accident."

"That was not an accident. He got arrested in a drug deal gone bad."

"Do you honestly believe that? He didn't even do drugs back then and you know it."

"He's always loved living on the edge, so drugs weren't a far leap. There's a first time for everything, and obviously that night—"

She held both palms up to cut him off. "Wrong. So wrong. He got arrested because Phoebe and I made stupid mistakes. He got arrested because he punched a cop trying to get to me. There were no drugs involved. Did you ever ask him about it?"

His chair creaked as he shifted position. "No."

"You just jumped to conclusions like I did. I thought he didn't want to see me ever again. That he hated me because he didn't defend me to you. But I've figured something out. Maybe he's the one who needs defending."

"Of all the people in the world who don't need defending, it's Chance Anderson," he said, voice muffled, maybe by his hands.

She crossed her legs and relaxed back against the cushions. "Do you know he can read braille? He learned it so he could understand me better. Can you read braille, Walter?"

"No."

"He came to my graduation. Did you come?"

Agitation tinged his tone. "So this entire push for independence is all about Chance Anderson."

"No." But it was because of him. He'd given her the power to finally break free. She uncrossed her legs and gripped her knees. "This is about me. *Me*, Walter. I want your power of attorney over me revoked. You guys did that when I was eighteen, and I was still so codependent and brainwashed I went along with it. But I'm not a lemming jumping off a cliff anymore."

She dug the paper folded in quarters out of her jacket

pocket and held it out toward him. He didn't take it, so she flattened it on the table between them. "I printed out a revocation form I found online and signed it. I want you to sign it, too." She pulled a pen out of her pocket and slammed it down on top of the paper. "I want control of my bank accounts and the money Granny and PawPaw left for me."

Heart hammering, she scooted to the edge of the sofa until her knees touched the coffee table. "I want to call you to chat, not because I have to check in at prescribed times. I want to sit down at dinner with you, Mom, and Dad and talk about something other than how we can adjust my accommodations to increase my safety. I want to meet up for pizza, not a lecture."

When he remained silent, she leaned forward. "I want my big brother back."

The air moved as he stood. Defeated, she slumped against the soft leather of the sofa. She'd said everything she knew to say, and it hadn't worked. That would mean getting a lawyer, which she was willing to do, but had hoped wasn't necessary.

Across the room a drawer opened and closed, and still, her brother was silent. The sofa cushion tilted as he sat next to her.

"He texted me earlier today," Walter said. A scratching sound accompanied the rustle of paper. "Chance, that is. He wants to meet up with me tomorrow."

He placed something in her lap, and she explored it. "What's in the file?"

"Your insurance policies, bank information including the trust fund paperwork, my copy of the power of attorney, and the signed revocation form."

Stunned, she reached out toward him. She found his face and traced her fingers over a single tear drifting down his cheek, and all the resentment and anger she'd bottled up for years drained away in an instant.

"When did this happen?" he asked, taking her hands in his. "When did my baby sister grow up?"

"When you weren't looking. Hazard of sighted people."

He released her hands, and there was a pause before he spoke. "You love him, don't you?"

She couldn't help but smile. "I've loved Chance my whole life."

"He really wasn't buying drugs that night?"

"No. Wanna hear the story?"

"Do you still like sausage and mushroom pizza?"

"Yep."

His phone clicked as he dialed. "Tell me a story, Gen."

Chapter Twenty-Three

Chance was surprised that Walter had picked this bar when he confirmed their meeting by text late last night. He hung his raincoat over the back of a stool and ran his hands through his damp hair. Gen was still at work, but the memory of that first kiss in this bar affected him more than he'd anticipated. Heat and sadness blended in a painful ache in his chest.

He'd thought a lot about what Will had said on the pier, and he was right. Even though she needed to have the ultimate say, as a friend he should have always had her back.

"Hey, Doc. Good to see you." Andy, the bartender, placed a Dr Pepper in front of him. "You're not at your usual table."

"I'm meeting someone."

When he turned to check the door, he found Walter striding toward him, wearing his suit from work, expression grim. *Fuck*. This was going to be hard, but it was the right thing to do. No excuses, just facts.

After a stiff handshake, he introduced his former friend. "Andy, this is Walter Richards, Gen's brother."

The men shook hands, and Andy's blond eyebrows rose. "Ah. The big brother. Glad to meet you. Your sister's amazing." He placed a basket of pretzels in front of them and took Walter's order for a draft beer.

"Gen *is* amazing," Chance said, staring straight ahead as Walter settled onto his stool, leaning his umbrella against the dark wood of the bar. "Genny... Gen is extraordinary, Walter, and it's past time you realize exactly how special she is." He'd memorized this speech and had practiced it in his head for years now, but somehow, it didn't seem to flow like it did in his head.

He slid a glance over to find his friend staring openly at him, face neutral. Andy delivered the beer and moved to the far end of the bar.

"Gen's smart and capable and..." The speech seemed ridiculous to him now and didn't even come close to how he really felt, so he decided to ditch it.

A woman sat to his left and Andy took her order, glancing up when the bells on the door jingled.

"I love her, Walter. I've loved Genny since I saw her on that bench at T-ball practice when she was five years old telling her doll not to cry." A glance at his onetime friend revealed no reaction other than a raised eyebrow. "I love her... No. I don't just love her, I'm *in* love with her. You say I'm not worthy of her, but I'm trying to be. My whole life, I'm going to try to be."

Still, the man next to him said nothing. No anger, no rebuttal, nothing at all. Outside, thunder crashed and the bell on the door tinkled as people came in to escape the rain.

"What you've done is wrong. You can't take something you love and hold it to your chest, never letting it loose for fear it might get hurt. You told me I'm bad for her and that my sports and love of adrenaline will put her in danger, but you're wrong. I'd never intentionally put her in harm's way, but you have. In keeping Gen this close, *you* are hurting her. Let her make her own mistakes just like everyone else."

Walter propped his head on his elbow as if fascinated, which was unnerving.

"Let her go, Walter. She loves you, and if you let her fly, she'll come back. It's so hard to let go, I know. But it's the right thing to do."

"You don't seem to have much trouble letting her go. You've done it twice so easily."

He ran a hand through his hair. "Nothing. Absolutely nothing in this world has been harder than letting that woman go. But I'll never smother her. Because I love her, I can let her go, knowing it's the right thing to do. And you need to do the same. And maybe, just maybe, she'll come back to us. And you know what? If she does come back, we'll be the luckiest bastards in the world."

His phone vibrated in his pants pocket. It was probably Michael wondering why he wasn't at work. Nothing was more important than this conversation, so he let it roll over to voicemail.

"I didn't speak up both times, because I believed it was not my place. That Gen needed to fight her own battles in order to win them. But now, I think I made a mistake. Not because she needs a caretaker or a defender, but because she needs a friend. And that's what friends do. They get each other's backs. They believe in each other."

"That's what friends do?"

"Yes."

"What does a friend do when all the rumors and evidence show his friend to be something entirely different than what was originally believed?"

Where was he going with this? Chance's throat tightened and another roll of thunder sounded from outside. "You follow your gut and heart."

Chance met Walter's eyes.

"I haven't been a very good friend, then, have I, Chance?"

"No, you haven't."

Walter took a pull on his beer. "I've been a shitty brother, too, huh?"

"Your heart was in the right place."

He set his beer down and swiveled on his stool to face Chance. "When Genny came and talked to me last night, she said I needed to pull my head out of my ass and look around."

Chance laughed and picked up a pretzel. "Yeah, that too." His heart kicked up a notch. She'd actually done it. She'd confronted her brother.

His phone buzzed again, and he let it roll over to voicemail. The woman next to him paid her tab and left.

"She also demanded full control of her finances."

"She can do that stuff herself. You know that, right?"

"I do now. She was very...direct. On more than one occasion before she left my place last night, references were made to shoving large objects up a specific orifice on my body."

Chance busted out laughing.

"I hadn't realized she was quite so passionate."

Passionate, yes. Passionate, giving...amazing. Chance took a sip of Dr Pepper to wash down the pretzel while Walter finished off his beer. "So, what do we do from here?"

"What do you want to do, Chance?"

"Well, I'd really like to spend time with your sister without having to kick your ass in order to do it."

"I'd really like to not get my ass kicked. She did a good enough job of that already. Do you plan on taking her with you on your crazy adventures?"

His phone rang again. *Fucking Michael.* He was supposed to be on his honeymoon. Without checking the screen he answered. "What the hell do you want?"

"You."

Genny.

There was a long silent pause where his heart hammered so hard, he was sure she could hear it over the line. "So, answer my brother's question. Are you going to take me with you on your adventures?"

"Yes, I…" *Thank God.* He sagged in relief and set his glass down. "Hell, yes."

"Hey, Doc!" Gen's brunette friend slid onto the stool next to him. Andy grinned and placed a beer in front of her. Before he could answer, his body buzzed to life with awareness. She was near. Without seeing her, he knew. He could actually feel her presence—just like Gen had described when they were younger.

He spun on his stool to find her only feet away, one arm extended in front, the other bent slightly to protect her face as she moved toward him.

Exactly like before.

The hood to her raincoat was tipped back and her wet bangs matted against her forehead. Before her fingers made contact, she stopped, and so did his heart. She tilted her head and took a deep breath through her nose.

"Walter."

"Gen."

And instead of the stiffness Chance had expected, both siblings smiled. They were in on this together. Walter hadn't picked this bar, she had.

"How long have you been standing there?"

She smiled, and his whole body became lighter. "Long enough to know you've got my back." And then, she did the most amazing thing. Just like before, she reached forward and touched his chest, then worked her way up his neck to his face while he held his breath.

He closed his eyes, reveling in the feel of her touch on

his face. Like before, she ran her thumb over his lip. And then she kissed him. Sweet and gentle at first, as if telling him everything was okay. Soon, the sweetness turned heated, and everything was better than okay. It was phenomenal, like her hands digging into the hair at the nape of his neck to pull him closer.

A whoop from her friend was followed by some applause and whistles from other bar patrons. She pulled back and grinned. A look over his shoulder confirmed Walter was grinning, too.

Tilting her head, she arched a brow. "So, you let me down, Anderson."

"I'm more than happy to try that again, Richards."

"I'm talking about the bucket list."

"On exactly which item did I let you down?"

"Well, certainly not on number ten," she said, looping her arms behind his neck.

Her friend snorted, then coughed as her beer went down the wrong way.

"We didn't finish the list," Gen said.

"No, we didn't." She moved with him as he slid off the stool. "And that was very remiss of me. Let's take care of that right now, shall we?"

The group of people huddled inside the door to escape the rain parted as he led her out. And right there, in the middle of the street, he took her in his arms. A cab honked as rain poured down. Wrapping his arms around her, he pulled her hard against his body and swayed in time to the music in his head. "I love you, Genny."

She stopped swaying and held his face in her hands, cars switching lanes to go around them in the pounding rain that had brought traffic to a near standstill. "I've loved you my whole life. Ever you since you took on those bullies at the ball field, and taught me to ice skate. Since you punched a cop to get to me… Since you gave me the power to stand up to my brother and take my life into my own hands."

"Kiss me, Genny."

And she did. From inside the bar, cheers erupted, and all around them, cars honked.

She pulled back and placed her hands on his face to feel his expression. "What do you see?"

He stared into her beautiful face, and with strangers cheering, and traffic honking, and the rain pouring down like forgiveness, he answered honestly. "My future."

Acknowledgments

Writing the Anderson Brothers series has been a delight, primarily because of the hard work, love, and brilliance of Liz Pelletier and all the folks at Entangled Publishing.

Getting these books to the readers is a team sport and I have a great team! Heartfelt gratitude to Candace Havens, Robin Haseltine, Heather Howland, Jessica Turner, Crystal Havens, and the entire Lovestruck and EP team.

A great deal of the boots-on-the-ground promo and pick-me-up encouragement came from members of my amazing Facebook group, Camp Clarke. Special thanks to Angela Bailey, Nicole Counts, Carolyn Downes, Connee Edstrom, Lucero Guerrero, Angela Guilherme, Bette Hansen, Evelin Hustis, Chris Jones, Angela Kinney, Elois Lloyd, Kim Matlock, Virginia Mayer, Bube Petreska, Yazmin Rangel, Danielle Salley, Christine Karper-Smith, and Tiffani Storck for beta reading, proofing, and/or throwing ideas around with me.

I could not have made it through the end of the first draft without Shawna Stringer and Deanna Lynn. Love beyond words, ladies.

And big hugs and love to Sophie Jordan, Nicole Flockton, Lily Dalton, Patrick McDonald, and Lynn Lorenz for the brainstorming and kicks in the backside.

Thank you Laine, Hannah, Emily, and Robert. Look up "love" in the dictionary, and there's a picture of you.

Last, but always first, thank you to all the readers who have fallen in love with the Anderson brothers right along with me.

About the Author

Marissa Clarke lives in Texas, where the everything is bigger, especially the mosquitoes.

When not writing or reading, she wrangles her rowdy pack of three teens, husband, and a Cairn Terrier named Annabel who rules the house (and Marissa's heart) with an iron paw. If you love young adult fiction, be sure to check out Marissa's alter ego, Mary Lindsey!

www.marissaclarke.com
Join Camp Clarke for news and insider information!

Discover the Anderson Brothers series

SLEEPING WITH THE BOSS

NEIGHBORS WITH BENEFITS

Also by Marissa Clarke

DEAR JANE

THREE DAY FIANCÉE

LOVE OUT LOUD

ACCIDENTALLY PERFECT

ACCIDENTALLY FAMOUS

LOVE ME TO DEATH

Find love in unexpected places with these satisfying Lovestruck reads...

THE BEST MAN PROBLEM
a novel by Mariah Ankenman

The last time Lily hooked up with someone in a wedding party, it nearly cost her her wedding planning business. Fortunately, those rules don't apply to handsome strangers. Unfortunately, after a shared night, the handsome stranger turns out to be the best man in the upcoming wedding she's planning. Lincoln has four short weeks before the wedding to convince Lily there's something more between them. And that love is something you can never plan.

FINDING MR. RIGHT NEXT DOOR
a Firefighters of Station 1 novel by Sarah Ballance

For Lexi, burning down her kitchen was disaster enough. Agreeing to move in with her sexy as sin, totally off-limits best friend until her house is livable again? Utter madness. They already share everything—their jobs, their friends, their backyard, even their dog. Lexi refuses to risk losing any of it by giving into the sudden, intense sexual attraction sparking between them. But some fires burn out of control, and the one between her and Matt just might be unavoidable.

LOVE OUT LOUD
an Animal Attraction novel by Marissa Clarke

Veterinarian Fiona Nichols does not do well in stressful social situations. But that doesn't stop her from checking out the delectably hot guy in her building...from afar. Fate apparently has a nasty sense of humor, though. Turns out that Jake Ward is Fiona's new public-speaking coach. A hot extrovert who always knows what to say. And now she's finally getting out of her comfort zone...only to get in over her head.